TAAQTUMI
VOLUME 2

Published by Inhabit Media Inc.
www.inhabitmedia.com

Inhabit Media Inc. (Iqaluit) 2434 Paurngaq Cres., Iqaluit, Nunavut, X0A 2H0
(Toronto) 612 Mount Pleasant Rd., Toronto, Ontario, M4S 2M8

Copyright © 2025 Inhabit Media Inc.
I Wouldn't Miss Them © 2025 Jessie Conrad; Maniittuq © 2025 Aviaq Johnston; Mask &
Bone © 2025 Jamesie Fournier; I Am Enough © 2025 Rachel and Sean Qitsualik-Tinsley;
Taaliqtuq © 2025 Malcolm Kempt; Watch It! © 2025 Gayle Uyagaqi Kabloona; Saatapiaq ©
2025 Terrie Kusugak; The Power Outage © 2025 Micah Silu Inutiq; Utiqtuq: Chapter 2 © 2025
Gayle Uyagaqi Kabloona

Photography: Alex Linch/Shutterstock.com, Alexandra P.P/Shutterstock.com, ambquinn/
Shutterstock.com, andysavchenko/Shutterstock.com, BW Isolated/Shutterstock.com,
CeltStudio/Shutterstock.com, CemoLmages/Shutterstock.com, Drakuliren/Shutterstock.com,
Ene Diana/Shutterstock.com, Ivan Kurmyshov/Shutterstock.com, Jakub Krechowicz/
Shutterstock.com, Karuntana999/Shutterstock.com, Katrien1/Shutterstock.com,
Khe1shoots/Shutterstock.com, Krasovski Dmitri/Shutterstock.com, Leigh Prather/
Shutterstock.com, lisevich ruslan/Shutterstock.com, m-agention/Shutterstock.com,
Marcin Perkowski/Shutterstock.com, MIND AND I/Shutterstock.com, POUSSINFRANCAIS/
Shutterstock.com, Raggedstone/Shutterstock.com, Siwakorn1933/Shutterstock.com,
s_oleg/Shutterstock.com, sruilk/Shutterstock.com, Thorben Hartmann/Shutterstock.com,
tofutyklein/Shutterstock.com, Tyler Olson/Shutterstock.com, Vishnevskiy Vasily/Shutterstock.com

Editors: Neil Christopher, Kelly Ward-Wills, Anne Fullerton
Art director: Danny Christopher

All rights reserved. The use of any part of this publication reproduced, transmitted in any form
or by any means, electronic, mechanical, photocopying, recording, or otherwise, or stored in a
retrievable system, without written consent of the publisher, is an infringement of copyright law.

We acknowledge the support of the Canada Council for the Arts for our publishing program.

This project was made possible in part by the Government of Canada.

Printed in Canada

ISBN: 978-1-77227-583-4

Library and Archives Canada Cataloguing in Publication

Title: Taaqtumi. Volume 2.
Other titles: Taaqtumi (2025)
Identifiers: Canadiana 20250214539 | ISBN 9781772275834 (softcover)
Subjects: LCSH: Inuit—Canada, Northern—Fiction. | CSH: Horror tales, Canadian
  (English)—Canada, Northern. | CSH: Short stories, Canadian (English)—Canada,
  Northern. | LCGFT: Short stories.
Classification: LCC PS8323.H67 T332 2025 | DDC C813/.08738089719—dc23

TAAQTUMI
VOLUME 2

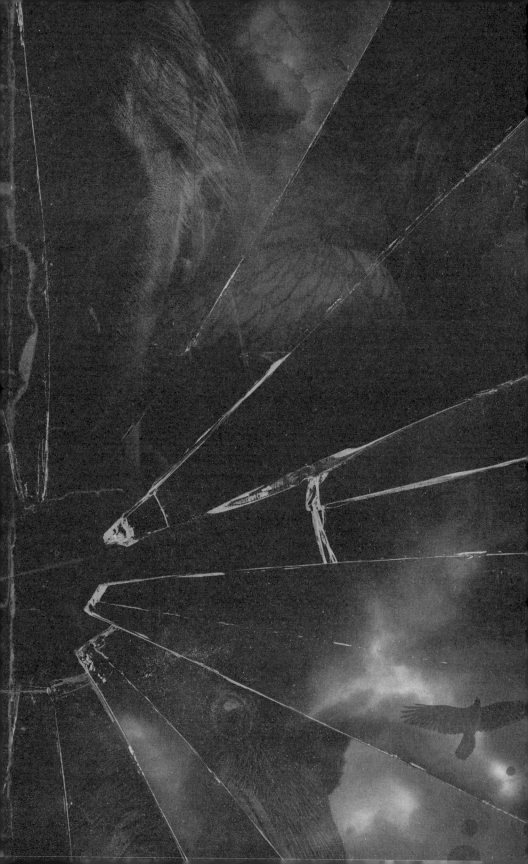

Contents

I Wouldn't Miss Them   1
Jessie Conrad

Maniittuq   17
Aviaq Johnston

Mask & Bone   27
Jamesie Fournier

I Am Enough   45
Rachel and Sean
Qitsualik-Tinsley

Taaliqtuq   85
Malcolm Kempt

Watch It!   91
Gayle Uyagaqi Kabloona

Saatapiaq   107
Terrie Kusugak

The Power Outage   125
Micah Silu Inutiq

Utiqtuq: Chapter 2   141
Gayle Uyagaqi Kabloona

Glossary of Inuktitut Words   153

Contributors   159

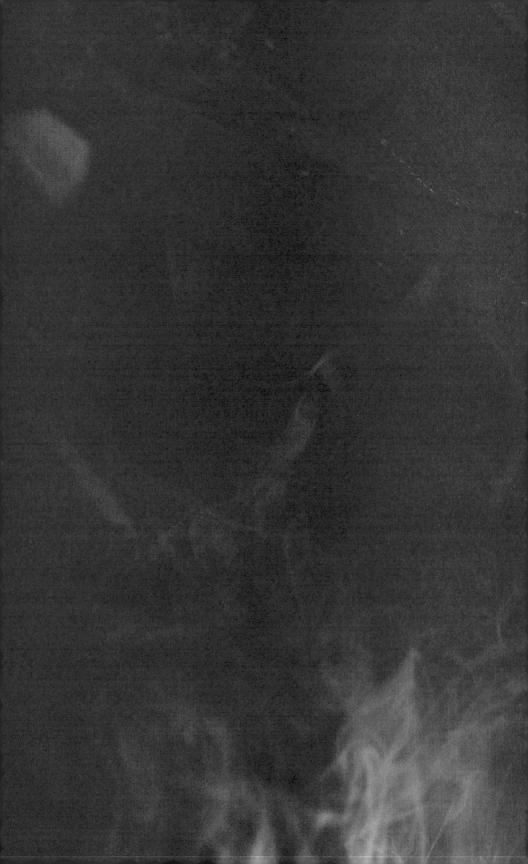

I Wouldn't Miss Them
Jessie Conrad

Trigger warning: This story contains descriptions of domestic abuse.

I WAS NINETEEN WHEN I MET RANDAL, THE SAME AGE AS you. He was in the returns section, exchanging an auger. He wasn't good at flirting, mostly mumbling and unable to look me in the eyes. I thought this meant he was the shy guy type, so was surprised that he offered me a ride home. To be honest, I only said yes because it was minus forty and he had a new truck. After exchanging numbers, he called every night. There was no one else pursuing me, so I talked to him mostly out of boredom. Never get involved with a guy just because you're bored, my girl. . . .

Anyways, I eventually caught feelings—*big feelings*. We talked for hours about nothing and everything. He made me feel like the centre of his world. Amka was my roommate at the time. She complained because her cousin that slept on the couch couldn't buzz into our apartment with the phone line busy. We lived in Polaris Heights, one of the roughest buildings in town. She suggested Randal pay for a second phone line; she was sick of having her cousin climb through our windows. He picked out a cordless phone from Roy's Radio Shack. *I'm that old.* Then he got me a fur scarf with matching mitts, a gold rope bracelet, stuff I couldn't buy on my own working minimum wage. Drilling at the mine, he could afford it. He really spoiled me at first. . . . Tired of wearing the same parka I had since junior high, I asked him to get me one of those puffy short jackets all the girls down south wore. It was bright pink, just like the heart-shaped box of chocolates and the dress from Northern Divine. I don't wear pink anymore.

Things got more serious. I started sleeping at his place on weekends, away from the paper-thin walls, three-day parties, and pounding music that kept me up all night. To this day I can't listen to the *Cowboys from Hell* album. Amka liked living at Polaris Heights just as much as I did, but we made the best of it. We comforted each other by laughing at the twisted things in life, like how the pipes froze after I bitched about all the dirty laundry we had, and the ravens that caused a power outage that forced us to eat half-cooked turkey in the dark. We had no flashlights or candles and gave ourselves food poisoning. We were pretty dumb back then. Most people are at that age, but hopefully you'll be the exception.

Sometimes the three of us would go out together, but that didn't last. After we had a few beers at Huskey's, he reached the conclusion that Amka was a bad influence on me, and that "women shouldn't act *that way.*" I asked what he meant; we were just having fun. The question resulted in bruises from my collarbone to my ribs. I'm sorry if this is hard to hear, my girl, but that's how it was. Don't get sad, your granny was lucky enough to live and tell this story. So . . . as it happened, my feelings for him stuck. I didn't want to love him, *but I just did*. It's like he cast a spell on me that robbed me of my dignity and worth. Does that make any sense to you?

Things didn't improve, they never do in those types of relationships. He grew more distrustful of Amka. I asked why—she's a good person and wouldn't do anything to put me in harm's way. "I heard she steals," was his answer. When my purse went missing, he pointed his finger at her, vibrating to the point I thought his skeleton would rupture from his skin. His face became twisted with rage, making him unrecognizable, ugly. . . . This wasn't the guy I fell for. I was foolish enough to believe him, until I found my purse stuffed between his truck console and seat, on top of a bra that wasn't mine. By this time, I figured it was too late to salvage my friendship with Amka, or to leave Randal. I was two months pregnant with your dad and his brother.

I moved with him to the Delta, to a community called Grayling Point, where he was originally from. We married shortly after. It was a small, private wedding—nothing to brag about. I didn't get to invite anyone because it was so short notice. Ah, if only I knew then what I do now. . . .

In the photos, Grayling Point looked quaint and friendly, the kind of place I could get accustomed to. I looked forward to a fresh start with him. But I soon learned that photos are deceiving. People weren't as welcoming as I thought they would be. I suspected it was because they judged me unfit to marry into such a traditional family. I wasn't traditional in any sense, and not because I didn't appreciate my heritage. I never really had the opportunity to learn anything cultural because your great-grandparents died when I was six. After that I was raised in foster homes in the city. If you could call Yellowknife a city. The few traditions I practised were making offerings to the land and water before travelling, and to animals after a successful hunt, things I faintly remembered.

Unlike other women in Grayling Point, I barely knew how to sew and didn't speak Inuvialuktun or Gwich'in. But I was willing to fit in. At the sewing groups I would nod and smile at the chattering wives who said things I couldn't understand, redo the beadwork on Randal's moccasins until it looked perfect. It never was.... The only person who I genuinely felt welcomed by was a woman who gave me needles when mine broke. The sewing group was short-lived—he preferred me at home.

Back then, everyone watched over each other, they were taken care of. Relatives made deliveries to the elderly, hunters packed community freezers, and people visited each other every day. My experience was far different though. I was isolated and stalked in my own home. He didn't let anyone visit, only his parents every few months. No matter where I was, he watched me. In the kitchen where he criticized my cooking, the bathroom when I was having a soak, in our bed when I was trying to dream, him stinking like cigarettes and whiskey. One time while I was walking down the stairs, I could feel him staring. He tripped me from behind, saying it was an accident, that I used too much cleaner and made the stairs slippery. My left incisor has since been replaced. My girl, I'm sorry if this is hard to hear. If you want me to stop, just say so. We can talk about something else....

I held onto the hope that he would turn back into his former self. The truth was, his former self never existed; that was just a character he invented to hide his true nature. What Randal is, or was, is something I still can't explain. There are a lot of things in this life I can't explain. Like how during our first hunting trip he carried the biggest bull I've ever seen like it was nothing while dragging a cow. The weight should have broken his back. We had two sleds; one was mostly empty. This is where I thought he would put them. He told me to unfold the tarp. I wasn't finished when he flung the caribou down, started using the saws and knives with more force than necessary, partitioning flesh from bone, life from death. No animal deserves to be treated that way, not even when they're dead. He laughed when blood spattered on my face. I told him to make an offering, to give thanks. He ignored me like I was a ghost. I couldn't stomach being next to him, so I went for a walk and did it myself. I buried my gold bracelet in the snow. I had no tobacco. Plus, I didn't want it, it was just something he used to lure me in. It was quiet out there, away from him. Peaceful, perfect . . . until it happened.

At first, they sounded like faint whispers, but then became louder, saying my name. *They* could be a number of things, I don't claim to know what they are, just that they were there and calling my name. They sounded like they were coming from the opposite direction from where Randal was, in the west. We were the only ones way out there, though, from what I could see. "Go" was the last word they said. I knew what they meant, for me to leave him. I wanted to ask them how—I was pretty helpless back then. But then he yelled for me to return.

So, this was our first hunting trip, and the only time we cut up meat together. After that, he left the task up to me, no matter what time of day or night, despite having newborn twins to feed and a house to keep clean. One night he woke me up at 4 a.m. I had countless sleepless nights; he didn't make things easier for me. He could have asked others to help but chose not to. After three years of this, I began fainting. I asked him what he thought about hiring a nanny, or putting the boys in daycare, since I couldn't do everything on my own and wanted to find a job. He ignored me, and told me to get him a second plate of ribs. I held in my anger, knowing that throwing the plate would do me no favours. I had to stay able-bodied. Your dad and uncle were growing fast, it was getting harder to keep up with their busy bodies even without injuries.

But my health was inevitably failing. The anemia was severe enough that most days were a struggle to get out of bed. I was regularly exhausted and looked even worse. I put on concealer to hide the dark circles under my eyes that would be sweated off by noon. Then, no longer caring how I looked, I threw out my makeup. He called me haggard, told me to make myself pretty again. If there's one thing I learned from him, it was how to use selective hearing. I wasn't his trophy wife anymore, so didn't have to look like one.

After giving myself a concussion from fainting on the fireplace, I went to the clinic. The nurse prescribed me iron pills. Too bad for me they didn't help as much as I needed them to. Intravenous treatment was the next option, which I had to fly to Yellowknife for. I didn't want to leave your dad and uncle with Randal, but had no choice. The doctor ran tests on me for what seemed like forever, deciding it was best that I stay in the hospital until I stabilized. I was all sorts of hurt. . . . Each day I felt stronger, but also lonelier for my kids. When I called to talk to them, he would say they were busy playing with the puppies or visiting his parents in Inuvik. After two weeks he stopped answering my calls.

I began envying other patients who had visitors. They brought fresh flowers, teddy bears, all the cute get-well gifts. One of the women I shared a room with gave me a yellow rose from her bouquet. It was the nicest thing anyone had done for me in a while.

I ordered myself carnations, trying to create the illusion I had a loving marriage like the others. They were mouldy and wilted by the time they arrived. I was raring and ready to go home.

He picked me up from the airport late. I was pissed off that he made me wait for so long and didn't bring your dad and uncle. As usual, he didn't look me in the eyes, telling me they were still at his parents' place and that it was "better for them there." It was something in the way he said *better* that really got to me. . . . What was more concerning, though, was that it was customary for the grandparents to raise the first-born. He said the boys had to stay together because they're twins, but not to worry because we would visit them during Christmas. And that we would have another baby soon. "It will be fine," he said. Separating me from my kids would hurt me more than his fists, that's why he did it. When he leaned in for a kiss, I did something I never thought I could do. I slapped him. Hard. Slamming on the brakes, he kicked me out of the truck. As he sped off, I laughed at my situation. No kids, no husband, no ride home, and maybe not even any hope. Have you ever felt that way before, my girl? Hopeless?

The laughs turned into tears. There was nothing funny about being ditched on the side of the road in winter. I didn't heed the old superstition that warns us not to cry outside at night or we'll attract evil spirits. If anything was going to take me, I thought, *let it*. I was at my worst here. It was getting colder and darker by the minute. I wasn't anticipating walking home in jogging pants and an unlined jacket. Thankfully, someone pulled over. I recognized her from the sewing group—she was the woman who gave me the needles. Before dropping me off she gave me her number, JAN 867-555-0121. She still has the same number.

I slept downstairs that night in the kids' room, unable to bring myself to the same bed as him. In the morning, when the sun was rising, I started to pray. I didn't regularly pray back then, but it seemed like the right thing to do. Afterward I made coffee. This is when I heard them again, the voices from the hunting trip. I've learned in my old age that we all have protectors. Some of us can see them, while others only hear them, which is what was happening to me. They said the same thing they did before, but with more fervency. I didn't need to be told a third time. . . .

But I still didn't know *how* to leave. I had my own money saved, not much, but enough for emergency situations. I couldn't use it though; he had my bank card. Luckily enough there was still the landline. When he left for the day, I called Jan.

I worked on the suit each morning for three days. I used white spray paint to lighten my jacket and snowpants and hung them up to dry in the kids' closet so he wouldn't see them. If he did see, he would figure out I was hiding something from him. He wasn't stupid, as much as I wanted him to be. After the paint dried, I sewed pieces of green and brown kitchen rags onto the fabric. It was a rough DIY job, but it did the trick. I had no other options for camouflage.

The puppies were whining. I gave them more kibble, put them in the kennel, and called Jan to pick them up so she could take them on her flight to Fort Res. She gave them to her sister, who ran one of the best dog teams in the NWT. They would have a good home. Even though he treated the puppies better than me, they were still vulnerable to his outbursts. I didn't feel comfortable leaving them with him. If I couldn't have my kids, he couldn't have his dogs, a wife, or a house. I was bent on revenge back then. I don't recommend it.

The explosion wasn't as loud as I predicted; two loud bangs before the plume formed. Black smoke hovered above my burning house, like it was expelling all the darkness that it harboured. Now, you understand why I made the suit; I couldn't risk anyone seeing me leave. On snowshoes I followed fluorescent tags tied onto branches that Jan left. I stuffed them into my pocket so nobody could follow where they led, to a rusty but intact snowmobile and jerry cans. There would be about ten miles of trail break before I would reach the old winter road not a lot of people used anymore, then a few hours to Tsiigehtchic, where I would catch a charter the next day to Yellowknife, courtesy of Jan, bless her soul for getting me a ticket. I would stay at the women's shelter and file for full custody. This was our plan. The idea to set the house on fire was all mine, though. I was a different person then, my girl.

Things didn't go as planned, though; they never do. The whistling gradually started, but the stench was with me the entire time. It smelled like carrion, heavy and rotten, making me gag. If hate had a smell, it would be that. I told myself it was a lone wolf, but knew better. It was a *nàhgq*, a bushman. I'm sure you've heard of them before. I *really* needed a gun at that point, but he kept them locked in a safe I couldn't crack. The only things I had were a few flares, a compass, IDs, some snacks, and a Thermos. I thought of using a flare to scare it off, but didn't want to expose my location. I always believed in them, but never in a million years thought I would encounter one. Some say they can be benevolent; others say they'll abduct you to eat or for other foul reasons I don't need to mention.

From my peripheral vision I caught a glimpse of it, crouching between the trees. Even then it was taller than me. I stopped myself from looking at it, although I wanted to.... Why is it that we want to see the things that scare us the most? I heard it move closer, twigs were breaking, it breathed heavily, stunk even more. I yelled for it to leave, trying to sound declarative, convincing. But instead I sounded scared shitless because I was. There was no one and nothing to help me. I never felt so alone. It started talking to me in the voices of my parents, Randal, Amka, even your dad and uncle, telling me to turn around, to stop. I covered my ears, pressed down on them as hard as I could, but still heard it, like it was inside my head. If I was a skeptic, I would have thought I was losing my mind, that none of it was real. But isn't your own mind working against you worse than crossing paths with a bushman?

"Adele, come on, girl, it's me!" it said in Amka's voice. I couldn't move, the fear totally consumed me. It was like my body was made of boulders. I told myself I had come too far to be stopped now, that I would live to be an old, old woman and watch my sons grow into the men they are today. Slowly, I regained control of my limbs and ran as fast as I could. I guess that's the secret, eh? If you're stubborn enough, you can do anything.

The adrenalin rush washed away my remaining fear. I felt . . . unfuckwithable. Now it was still following me, but more so out of curiosity. Soon the footsteps faded from earshot. Why it didn't take me, I'll never know. While plucking the last tag, I saw scattered pieces of metal and rubber on the snow. It was the spindles and skis from the snowmobile. The creature demolished my ride.

I crumbled inside, cursing Jan and everything else that convinced me to leave. I considered going back. There was insurance, we could rebuild our house. I could play nice and get him to bring your dad and uncle home, or just get them myself. . . . But I'm not one for long-term fantasy thinking. One word came to mind—*delusional.* Your granny was delusional to think she should go back to him. So, I did what I did before: I kept going. I would use the flares once I reached the old winter road, head to Tsiigehtchic as planned. Someone was bound to see the lights. They had to. I couldn't die out there and leave my kids without their mother.

My jacket and snowpants were torn from branches. I didn't notice earlier because I was too focused on getting away. Then my jacket zipper broke. I wondered who I pissed off in a past life to deserve this. Cold air crawled deep into my skin, then over it, again and again. There's cold, then there's freeze-your-tits-off cold. I got hypothermia and blacked out for a little while. I don't remember taking anything off. People do that, it's normal, they get so cold they think they're hot.

Freddy—I think that was his name—he found me in my base layers with bluing lips in front of their cabin. His wife immediately started treating me, dressed me in furs, wrapped me in a sleeping bag with hot water bottles, and fed me broth. They knelt close to me; I could feel their bodies' warmth. I was slurring bad, telling them how I saw a family of caribou, one bull, two cows. The smaller cow nudged me upward, toward the direction of the cabin. "And that's how I found you!" I said, waiting for them to agree. But they were adamant there weren't any caribou, they would have seen the tracks. Freddy told me I didn't know what I was talking about because my brain was half frozen. It then dawned on me that I didn't need to convince them. Who cares if they didn't believe me? My life didn't depend on it. Still, I wanted to tell them more, like how I evaded the bushman, what it did to the snowmobile—everything but the whole *I burnt down my house and escaped my asshole husband and need to get my kids back* part. There's something about near-death experiences that make people want to tell the world what happened; it's the pride of survivors. That makes it hard to be humble. Instead, I passed out.

I don't know how long I slept for; it was too long, anyways, with the nightmare I had. I was on what looked like the Peel River, carrying your dad and uncle. It was sunny out, everything glowed and glittered. The weather turned, though, fast, as it often does. It started blizzarding. The boys began crying, poor things. Through an opening in the ice, Randal emerged, but not all at once—*piece by piece*. First it was one finger, then a hand, an arm, a shoulder, and finally his head and torso. He looked like he'd been dead for weeks ... skin necrotized and bloated open, showing slates of bone. It's something I've tried to forget, but it remains with me. He tried dragging us into the water, clawing and biting at my feet. I kicked him away and slipped, dropped the boys. They disappeared into the blizzard. I called for them as I was dragged into the water. Nearly submerged, I woke up.

I was back in the Yellowknife hospital. This time, though, I heard the real voices of your dad and uncle, of Amka. She was now working as a security guard there and was on shift when I arrived at emergency. She helped the boys onto the bed. Their faces were rosy and sticky with jam, smiling, like the last time I saw them. It didn't even seem real ... I think I might have been in shock. I hugged them tightly, promising them we would never be apart again.

My mother-in-law, sitting by the window with Randal's dad, interrupted us. "Adele, there was an accident." She said it without emotion. "He fell through the ice. His body isn't recovered yet." I held my hands, bandaged from frostbite, up to my mouth to stop me from saying how I actually felt, which she mistook for a widow's grief. Although Randal was experienced, he wasn't the most cautious person, especially if whiskey was involved. It doesn't take much to get distracted and forget to drive around the darker, thinner patches of ice. Even then, his parents didn't comfort me, never liking me much anyways. That was okay, I wouldn't miss them, or their son. "Make that *accidents*, Adele, with the house fire that you'll have to sort out." I couldn't stand the way she talked. . . . A nurse came in, visiting hours were over. While walking out, his father said they were too old to take care of the boys and something about funeral arrangements.

I must have had one of those thousand-yard stares on my face. Amka asked if I needed anything. I told her nope, I have my boys and best friend back, *I have everything I need*. It was the right time to apologize for taking sides. She easily forgave me, offered us the spare room in her new apartment. Of course I took it. Although I was right back where I started, there was nothing wrong with that.

After the boys fell asleep, we smoked a joint behind the hospital. Soon, probably the next day, I figured, I would have to talk to the RCMP and insurance company. My script would be true enough. Randal had a habit of leaving the fireplace door open, he was also a smoker. I left when he was still home, getting ready to go fishing. . . . But before all that could happen, I had to decompress.

I reflected on the past few years, on the kind of marriage I had. Amka said she had a feeling that's how it would go when she met Randal. I then spilled everything. I had to tell someone. I'm not good at keeping secrets, but she is. . . . Anyways, she started shaking

I Wouldn't Miss Them | 13

her head, I was afraid she thought I went too far. She didn't, though, she was in awe that I left Randal, burnt down the house, and almost froze to death, just for him to drown the same day. What are the chances? All I could say was that life will always be full of mystery and surprises.

So, this is why, my girl, Amka and Jan are my best friends. Can you get me another cup of tea? I have one more story to tell.

Maniittuq
Aviaq Johnston

The ride to the cabin was long, but leisurely. It was mostly smooth, with only one patch of rough packed tidal ice, which was reasonably maneuverable with the snowmobile. Once through the treacherous trail, there was a long climb up a steep hill, then a long winding trail down. After that, it flattened and straightened out for forty kilometres or so, through the valleys of rolling, rocky hills.

There was only one area where Saa hesitated, and parked the snowmobile for a moment to gather her bearings. It was a channel in which the current was strong and the ice rarely formed thick enough in various areas, sometimes making it difficult to spot. Just on the other side of the channel was Maniittuq, a gorgeous bay interspersed with small islands and an abundant river flowing with Arctic char. Saa and her father had gone through this area many times together, it was unavoidable—the last stretch before finally reaching the cabin—but it was her first time going alone.

She could see her father's trail from the day before, slightly windswept but easy enough to follow. They had discussed this part of the journey quite extensively, going over it in meticulous detail to ensure Saa would feel confident in her passage; what she should do when she reached the channel, what signs to keep an eye out for, to be vigilant, and to take deep breaths before proceeding.

Saa looked around, spotting animal tracks close by. She walked over to them to try to recognize what animal had created them. As easy as second nature, she knew that they were polar bear tracks. The area was teeming with the animals. She squinted her eyes—there was something odd about them.

With closer inspection, she could make out the tracks of another animal inset with the bear's tracks. These she was more unfamiliar with, and she racked her brain for what they could be. Not big enough to be a wolf, but larger than a fox, something in between.

It took a moment for her to pinpoint it. *Qavvik*! A wolverine.

A chill ran over her spine. She'd been told stories about this area since her father had decided to build his cabin here, many of which involved a wolverine roaming the area, and a woman screaming or crying from over the hillsides or roving the shoreline and preying on those who crossed her path. Many of the stories led to the belief that the wolverine and the woman were synonymous with one another.

On top of that, the polar bear tracks were deeply concerning. They were fresh. The cabin had been standing for five years now, and it was notoriously known for being broken into by polar bears at least two or three times a year. Sometimes more. Despite the door and windows getting boarded up with plywood every time they left, and all traces of food and trash being brought home at the end of every visit. They'd often return to find the sheets of wood flung off or askew, the door opened wide, and the cabin slowly filling with snow.

Worry spread into Saa's belly, and she got back on her snowmobile to finish the journey. She realized that she hadn't contacted her father on the VHF radio before heading out. The last she'd heard from him was the night before, when he let the family know that he'd made it safely to the cabin.

Her father had left after work yesterday, taking an extra day off for the spring long weekend. Saa, on the other hand, felt like she couldn't take the time off, after missing several days due to hangovers and other sicknesses that were more likely due to the lethargy of depression than anything else.

Now, she just wished she'd gone ahead with him. Would she have gotten fired? Probably not. Just another fact-finding meeting with HR, a slap on the wrist, disappointment from her coworkers and supervisors, but nothing drastic.

Her worry propelled her forward. She sped through the channel at full speed, noticing the slushy patches of ice at the last minute and swerving around them. She made it to the end of the channel fine, if a little panicked, her heart racing.

The journey ended with a last bend around a small peninsula, and in the little bay, the cabin rested on a plateau on the hill. Maniittuq was named for the rough terrain across the range of hills throughout the area. There was very little tide here, so the pack ice was easy to traverse and drive through. She could see her father's snowmobile parked next to the cabin, but no smoke wafting from the chimney. The plywood had been taken off the windows and safely leaned against the cabin, not torn off by bears.

Maniittuq

But as she closed the distance, her angle on the cabin changed and she could see the cabin door opened wide.

"Dad!" She yelled. "Dad?"

No answer. *Maybe he's gone on a walk over the hill? Maybe he just didn't close the door properly? Maybe it was too hot inside and he needed to cool down?*

But as she shut her machine off, there was a deafening silence.

"Dad?"

There was no reply.

Saa swung her rifle off her shoulder and loaded it, switching off the safety, and rushed into the cabin. It was freezing inside, the diesel heater gone cold. Snow had been trailed in by an obviously gigantic creature. Supplies were strewn about, her father's grub box and cooler torn apart, bits of the foam mattress littered, the Colman stove bent out of shape and leaking naphtha. An old can of Pepsi left on the floor with holes as big as thumbs bitten into it by fangs that could rip a human body apart.

No blood. So maybe her father was out hunting by foot. His rifle was gone, too. She lowered her own rifle.

She spotted the VHF and grabbed hold of the mic. "Elena, *tusaaviit?* Elena, are you listening?" But there was only static on the line. She spoke into the mic again, "*Tusaqsauvungaa?* Can you hear me?"

There was only static. Saa didn't understand the contraption well enough to know whether the signal was not working or if it was just that nobody was listening. Perhaps the wind or bear had jostled the antenna or wires outside? She didn't even know if that was something the VHF needed, her father had always been there to fix it if something was wrong. The skills to figure out what was wrong were not in her wheelhouse.

She marched back outside, screamed, "DAD!" only to hear her voice echoed back.

Saa slung her rifle back over her shoulders, unstrapped her pack from the back of her snowmobile, and brought it inside. She started the diesel heater to start warming up the cabin, took off her parka, and went through the bag, taking out a granola bar and scarfing it down. Underneath her parka, she was wearing a light down-filled coat, and her bib-style overall snow pants were tucked into warm boots. She grabbed extra bullets, stashing them in one of her many pockets.

She left the cabin to keep warming up, checked the ground for tracks, and found her father's footprints, as well as the meandering tracks of the polar bear following. She marched off in pursuit.

The tracks of both her father and the bear led uphill to high ground. This made sense to Saa—if she hadn't found the footprints, she'd have gone this way anyway. Intermittently, she called out for her father, but never heard a reply. It was eerily quiet, no birds peeping or flying.

At the top of the hill, the wind grew stronger. Saa gazed over the horizon and down the valley, but both her father and the bear were out of sight. Again, she could see the tracks of the two, and she started to follow them.

It was then that she heard the distant sound of a woman crying behind her. Saa stopped, felt the breath catch in her chest. Carefully, she took her rifle from its place slung over her shoulders, and slowly turned around.

Only to see that there was no one there. The sounds of the crying stopped.

For a moment, unbreathing, Saa stood still. Could the sound

have been made by a distant bird? But the silence was palpable, as if she had walked into a cloud of nothingness. She opened her jaw, trying to pop her eardrums, to no avail. Holding her breath, she kept making the motions, opening her mouth wide and pushing. The moment of quiet cleared, and she could hear the wind again. She let out a breath and she could hear that, too.

Then another sudden sound. A gunshot, from the direction of her father's tracks.

An alarm set off in Saa's head and she swung herself around, only to see a woman in an old fashioned *amaut* in the middle of the path. With a gasp of terror, Saa shot the rifle at her, but the image of the woman only faded as Saa fell backward into the snow. Her chest heaved, and she looked around frantically in search of the woman.

It was a long time before she calmed herself down, sitting up in the snow. There was still no sign of the woman she'd seen.

Then it all came back to her—the gunshot from the direction her father and the polar bear had travelled. She picked herself up, trying to forget what she had seen, focused only on reaching her father.

She sprinted down the hill, her gun poised in her arms, still loaded with the safety off. Soft patches of snow skewed her balance and she sunk to her knees, her momentum slowed.

The woman's cries were behind her again. Saa did not check, although the crying did not seem as distant as it had earlier. Of all the stories she'd heard of this area and the crying woman, none of them had violent or concerning ends, only the lingering feelings of creepiness. No children had been successfully stolen by the crying woman, no one lured to their death. She only ever knew the end of the stories to be of the woman disappearing for long bouts of time and returning occasionally.

"Go away!" Saa yelled, but the crying only grew louder and closer, as if the one making the sound suddenly was behind her. She swore she felt breath on the back of her neck, and Saa swung around, but there was nothing behind her.

When Saa turned back again, the woman was there. She was still filled with terror at the sight, but Saa didn't shoot this time. She stared at the woman's clothing, recognizing now that the amaut she wore was made from wolverine fur. Again, the image of the woman faded.

Saa made her way again, running more carefully, stepping only where the hard snow could bear her weight. Behind her, the woman's cries were no longer the pitiful sobs of a woman's grief. She could make out words now.

"*Taikungaunngilluti!*" and "*Utirululaurit!*" and "*Upanngillugit!*" and "*Taima!*" "Don't go there!" and "Go back!" and "Don't approach them!" and "Stop!"

Saa tried to continue ignoring the woman's cries, but she hesitated. The stories she'd heard about Maniittuq were often ambiguous, of no real consequence. To her, they had always been anecdotes told by boisterous children for shock value. Once, she was told by a friend that their cousin had seen a blue womanly figure on the shoreline when their family had gone camping here one summer. Another story she'd been told by her high school classmate was that they had seen their brother walking hand in hand with a similar womanly figure, but once they called out to the boy, the woman disappeared and their brother was dazed, without memory.

Saa kept her pace quick-marching down the hill, deep in thought, not acknowledging the cries still lingering behind her.

Maniittuq

Ghost stories were commonly shared amongst children and teenagers, but "ghost" wasn't the proper term for most of the beings she'd learned about in her culture. Saa turned the words over and over in her head. They were a warning. What beings warned humans back? She could only think of *tarriaksuit* possibly fitting the description, known to her as a peaceful race of beings who lived invisibly.

By the time she reached the valley below, her chest felt hot and painful, her throat dry in a way that no amount of water could quite quench.

She keeled over for a moment, chest heaving. Only a moment to catch her breath before continuing. The woman's cries had faded by now, perhaps sanctioned only on the hillside. She couldn't be sure about the boundaries of spirits, but she often thought that certain spirits stayed confined to one area. In any case, the return of silence was welcome as Saa continued forward.

Why had her father gone so far on foot? Why wouldn't he have used his snowmobile?

She followed the trail onward, a long stint without a sound or sight, just her and the path of her father and the bear before her. Finally, she yelled once again, "Dad!"

But as her echoes faded, she heard again only the whimpering behind her. The sound brought the chill back down her spine, an uncomfortable sigh throughout her body. She continued forward, picking up her pace.

The further she walked, the faster she moved, the crying only became louder and more urgent. Heaving, pathetic sobs, the kind that were inconsolable, ugly sounds. Saa squeezed her eyes shut and tried to cover her ears, but holding the rifle one handed was too heavy and awkward and her head wouldn't stop ringing.

"Stop!" Saa shouted, swinging herself around.

Again, there was no one. The sounds of the cries cut off in the middle of a disgusting, rattling sob.

Hoping the silence would linger once more, Saa turned back to her path, expecting again to see the woman.

But it was not the woman who stood before her this time. It was a snarling wolverine, lunging toward her.

Panicked and off balance, Saa shot her rifle square at the wolverine, and the bullet passed through the animal as it faded into nothingness, just as the crying woman had. The bullet, instead, landed into a man's back.

Saa's ears rang from the shot and she stared at the man as he toppled forward. Stunned, she remained motionless as she kept her eyes on him, willing for his image to disappear as the crying woman's and the wolverine's had, but he stayed there, unmoving.

"Dad?"

Just as before, there was no response.

Her senses returned, a cry bubbled up her throat, "Dad!"

Rushing forward, she found her dad's toppled body, a knife in his hand that he'd been using to butcher the polar bear that had stalked him. She shook his body, but his eyes were open, staring lifelessly at the sky.

Mask & Bone
Jamesie Fournier

"Hey there, Ajak! Got you something."

A baseball cap slid over the twelve-year old's head. The boy smiled as he looked up at his funny uncle. He like being called "ajak," an Inuktitut kinship term that his uncle saved just for him. The boy took off the cap and looked it over. A Blue Jays insignia was stitched across the front.

"My favourite! Where'd you get it?"

"Oh, that!" The heavy-set Inuk man smiled as he sat down across from the boy. "I just thought it looked like ya."

Confused, the boy put the hat back on. It was a little small, but he didn't mind.

"My famous caribou stew is just about ready! Hunted it myself." The man stuck a thumb to his puffed-up chest. "Cooked it, too! And your mom made the bannock so you know at least that half'll be good."

The man snickered as he turned and gestured to his back. The boy jumped on and giggled as his uncle trotted down the hallway like a chicken. When they entered the kitchen, the uncle unloaded his passenger, pointed, then stood with a saluting arm. "Prisoner Igali for chowtime, ma'am."

"At ease, officer." The boy's mother smirked as she knelt down and kissed her son's head. She stood and turned to her brother. "Why don't you and our prisoner go wash up? Dinner will be ready soon." The mother placed her hands on her hips. "And I don't much appreciate you calling our home a prison, mister."

The man raised his arms as he and his nephew backed away. "Whatever you say, Warden. Just don't put us in the hole, eh?" A dish towel flew into the man's face.

"Go! Wash! Now!" The woman threatened with a spoon.

When the man and his nephew returned, the rich aroma of caribou stew permeated the house. On the stovetop, a brown gravy bubbled amongst cubes of tender meat. The fat had rendered, and the meat pulled apart like butter. Hunks of potato, onion, and carrot floated in the thick sauce. The boy drooled, eyeing the thick stew, yet when he saw his mother's crisp, golden bannock sitting on the counter, the scent of fresh baking overpowered him. Light and fluffy with an oven roasted crust, the boy walked past the stew and quickly grabbed a fresh piece. He pulled it apart and steam wisped into the air. He smeared a fat glob of butter over its surface and greedily devoured it.

"Save some for the rest of us, Ajak!" his uncle teased. The boy wandered, eyes closed, to his mother and put an arm around her waist.

"You can't blame him for having good taste." The mother laughed as she cuddled her son. She eyed the bubbling stew, sighed, then looked over to her brother.

The uncle replied, "Sure! Keep it up! You're both this close to having no stew at all."

"We don't need your stinking stew anyway!" the mother dared.

"Speak for yourself," the boy said, now beside the stove. He was a ball of energy. His eyes gleamed as he ladled himself a warm bowl. His mother scoffed, stepped forward, and lifted the hat off the boy's head. She then turned and removed her brother's ball cap as well. She looked him in the eye and spoke softly.

"It's time," she said as she slowly put her brother's hat into his hands. "No hats indoors, Unc," she mocked as she bit off a piece of bannock with a smile and sat down at the kitchen table.

"No hats, now? *Sheesh*. Remember it didn't used to be like this? When we'd go out camping? On the land, under the sky. *Palaugaaq* cooked right over the fire! *Mamaqtuq*!" The nephew looked to his uncle questioningly, wiping stew from his mouth.

"Pau-gaak?" The boy inquired through a full mouth.

The uncle rolled his eyes and sat down with his own bowl. "They teach you nothing in those schools of yours? Pa-lau-gaaq." He carefully enunciated each syllable. "It's what we called bannock *back in the day*."

"Oh, god. Don't get him started." The mother chuckled. "*Back in the day*, your hot shot uncle was the most annoying kid ever. Something he has not grown out of, I might add."

"Hey! You're lucky to have a kid brother like me! Keep things interesting." The uncle turned to his nephew and pointed with his spoon. "So, back in the day, eh? When you saw a nice big pile of bannock you'd say something like, 'Whoa! Who brought the *gaaq*?' And then you'd just dig in. Out on the land, nice full belly kept a smile on your face and then *bam*! You'd be back out there running around with all the other kids, all night long 'cause the sun'd never go down, eh? After a day or so, after the stew had been set, you'd have some more and it'd be the tastiest damn thing ever! Mamaqtuq!" his uncle exclaimed, smacking his lips and ripping into another piece of palaugaaq.

"But, back then, our aunty, your grand aunt, I guess? She made the stew different. She had this long stone pot she liked to use. It came from long, long ago. Back when Inuit used to carve their pots out of soapstone before metal and iron came around, eh? She took real good care of it, only used it for special occasions. She'd roast the stew all day long under her big *qulliq*, her stone lamp. It would sit and simmer and be the tastiest thing ever! And that stone lamp, it burned seal oil, y'see? Or bowhead oil, the real flammable stuff. She'd burn that thing end to end all bright and beautiful and the heat'd be baking off your face it was so hot! Remember, Sis?"

"I remember you always coming back for seconds and thirds like a little monster and aunty'd have to shoo you off so there'd be enough to go around." The mother smiled as she wiped her bowl. "Something you and your nephew may have in common, I might add." The boy turned to his mother, who gave him a sly look.

"Well, I was hungry!" the uncle exclaimed as he clapped a hand across his belly. "I wanna live forever, y'know?"

"Well, you got enough there to last you the next few lifetimes at least," the woman needled. Her brother gasped dramatically. "Oh what, like you weren't beating your stomach like a big ol' drum just now—"

"That's *my* big ol' drum!" the man stated matter-of-factly as he ran his hands over his sizeable paunch. "How dare you, in front of the boy, no less. You know he looks up to me, eh?"

"He's gotta see past that gut somehow," the mother responded. The boy spat food back into his bowl as he tried not to laugh.

The uncle sat dumbfounded between his family members. "Ha, ha, ha," he mocked. "I come and make you guys good food and this is the thanks I get?"

The boy chuckled, careful not to let any more food escape his mouth. He brought a sleeve to his mouth. His mother batted away the arm and replaced it with a scowl and a paper towel.

"Now, you boys okay for the next little bit? I've got errands to run."

The uncle looked to his nephew. "Oh yeah, don't worry!" he stated, striking a huge palm against the boy's back as he swallowed. The boy's face paled as he gripped his throat. His uncle looked down, frowned, and then patted him harder once again. An oversized wad of meat tumbled across the table. His mother's wide eyes went from the meat to the boy and back again. The boy smiled wanly as his uncle spread out his arms. "What-I-tell-ya?" The uncle beamed. The mother ripped off another paper towel and threw it at the uncle.

"He gets it from your side of the family, y'know that, right?" she said as she grabbed her keys.

"It's the same family!" the uncle shouted as the door shut.

He turned to his nephew and rolled his eyes. "You eat up there, Neph." He dipped a hunk of bannock into his nephew's bowl and spoke while he ate. "It'll keep you out of trouble. Y'know Hansel and Gretel? Those kids out in the middle of the woods?" The nephew raised his eyebrows in agreement. "They find that candy house and lose their damn minds? You think those kids would have gotten into all that trouble if they had full bellies? No, sir! They'd be holding their big bellies, asleep and out of trouble!" His uncle closed his eyes and pretended to snore. A moment later he cracked open an eye.

"I remember they killed that witch!" his nephew spat out, happy with himself.

"Tricked her good! Right into that big ol' stove of hers!" The uncle cackled as he pictured the scene. His laughing trailed off as his eyebrows furrowed. "You ever wonder why she wanted to eat those kids? I mean, she's way out in the bush, there'd be moose, caribou, bears, or berries even! Lots much easier than waiting for some random kid to come wandering deep into the woods." The uncle paused and looked at the boy. "I mean, if I was trying to catch a kid, I wouldn't make a candy house way out in the middle of nowhere. That's just bad hunting!" The uncle slapped his knee and rocked himself into another fit of laughter. The boy laughed warily. He had pictured the candy house many times, the icing and candy canes and peppermints. Gingerbread you could sink your teeth into.

"But my aunt, she was my favourite, eh? She looked after us kids good, your mom, me, and our cousins. She's actually your namesake—Igali! That's why I call you Ajak! It means Aunt. So, you see, you may be my nephew but you're also my auntie." The uncle chuckled before he continued. "Igali is an old word, means kitchen, I think? Something like that." The man pushed the thought away. "Boy, Igali would make us good food in her big ol' stone pot she'd lug around everywhere. But one thing she didn't let us do is go off wandering into the damned woods alone!" The uncle tightened his lips and shook his head. His nephew parroted and rocked his head side to side.

"We moved around a lot back then. That's the way it used to be. Out on the land, you follow where the food goes, hm? Us kids be runnin' around having a heck of a time but ol' Igali she'd yell after us like, 'You kids don't go too far! Or the *amautaliit* will get you!'"

The uncle stopped and bared his teeth and growled. His nephew sat still, unphased. The uncle dropped his shoulders in bewilderment.

"So, what? Your mom never told you about the amautaliit?" The boy shook his head. "Well, she probably didn't wanna scare ya, that's all." The nephew's eyes widened as he felt a story coming on. The boy quickly stood, rinsed his bowl, put it in the dishwasher, and kicked it closed. "Another thing we didn't have! Dishwashers! Bah! We'd have to go down to the river to get water and drag it all the way back uphill. Then make a big fire to warm it up! You kids got it so easy these days you don't even know." The boy returned to his seat and rolled his eyes. When his uncle got worked up this was something he heard all too often.

"Were the amautaliit monsters?! Were they gross like *The Walking Dead* zombies?!" The boy struggled to contain his excitement.

"W-what?" his uncle stammered. "Where'd you see that?"

"TV!" The boy brightened. His uncle furrowed his eyebrows as the boy's mouth quieted and tightened to a fine line. The nephew's gaze shifted side to side as he avoided eye contact. His uncle raised an eyebrow as he rubbed the back of his neck.

"Well, the amautaliit, they lived way out on the land, eh? Out in the Wastes. That's what we called 'em back in the day, the Wastes, 'cause there was just nothing out there. Out there, the amautaliit be just waiting to scoop children up that weren't with their families. So, when we'd go get water, we'd go in groups of three or four. The amautaliit were supposed to have great big hoods, *amautiit*, like the one your mom carried you around in when you were a baby. That's where their name comes from, those parkas with the great big hoods." The boy nodded enthusiastically. Many women around their small northern town carried their little ones in beautifully ornate homemade parkas. Little babies peered out from the large hoods, eyes wide, cheeks fat and pudgy.

"So, if you were out too far, the amautaliit would grab you and put you in their parkas and steal you away! Forever and ever! Never seen again. *Poof!*" The uncle's words hung in the air. A twisted look washed over his face. He breathed quietly before he continued. "We'd hear about them, from time to time, out there, travelling, we'd come across other camps and families and hear that a child had gone missing, here and there. No explanation, no trace, no nothing." The uncle sat and pivoted the ball of his foot. His face darkened like a cloud before the sun. "I knew one of them. A kid I used to play with. He was a fun boy, his name was Eric, or something like that." The uncle laughed nervously. "Christ, so long ago, can hardly remember! But that's what they'd say, he went out on his own and the amautaliit got him." The nephew's breath stilled as his uncle dwelled.

"That's what they'd always say." The man looked away from the boy, his voice quivered. "I never wanted to believe it though! Bears, wolves, hell, even people, anything could have got him. Anything! Anything that wasn't the goddamned amautaliit!" The uncle spat out the words as he brought his hands to his eyes. He sighed and exhaled loudly. The nephew's heart sank to see his uncle so pained.

After a moment, the boy asked, "W-what happened?"

"Well, time went on, y'know?" The man sniffled. "We stopped travelling so much. We got what we needed from the stores, got houses in town, and we stopped hearing about the amautaliit and other what-have-yous." The nephew's head tilted. "Old Igali got a place down the street and your mom and I got to go over and play with all the cousins whenever we wanted." The uncle smiled widely, relief flooded his eyes. "We stopped hearing the old stories so much, but we kept to our ways. That's the one thing about us Inuks, eh? We're stubborn." The uncle pointed about the small house with his spoon. "You kids got your televisions and dishwashers and ughh, whaddayoucallthem . . . pod-casts?" The boy shrugged. "Well, whatever it is, it's still stories."

The man's voice quickened, his eyes wild in thought. "But that's how it goes, y'know? You gotta move with the tides. Adapt or die, that's what they say." The man blinked and his eyes lost their glassy shine. "Christ, where was I?" He shook his head and tapped his temple. "Sorry, kid. The old cracker barrel ain't what it used to be."

"Igali, down the street!" his nephew chimed.

"Oh right! Igali would make us her great stew on the stove and us kids would run about playing tag or hide-and-seek or whatever. Igali would yell at us to take it outside, but we never did, eh? More fun where it's not allowed," the uncle confided. A deep belch suddenly escaped the boy's throat. His uncle cackled and clapped his hands. "Nice! There ya go, neph! That's how you do it! Fill up your belly and let the food do its magic. Grab some more palaugaaq, it'll settle you down, and grab me another one while you're at it before your mom cuts us off, eh?" The boy wandered back with two pieces and sat back in his chair. "So, Igali would always be chasing us around, keeping us out of harm's way, eh? But another thing she didn't want us doing was going into her room. Where she slept. I mean most adults are like that. Parents gotta have a little peace and quiet, y'know?" The nephew nodded as he fondly remembered jumping on his mother's bed.

"So, one day I went into her room when she wasn't looking. She had a good closet for hiding in and I was determined not to let my cousin win another round. All the good places had been picked over, so I crept in there like a mouse, but something caught my eye." His uncle stopped and looked over his shoulders to see if anyone else was listening. His voice dropped.

"Now, Igali had some art on the wall, but that's the weird thing. That's all there was, there was nothing else but three small masks." The uncle stopped and stared at his nephew silently. He licked his lips as he shifted his gaze. "They were about the size of my palm." He held a hand toward his nephew's face. "And around each mask was a fur trim, like the ones we have on our parkas. Three little Inuk faces staring out of the wall." The boy's face wrinkled in confusion as he tried to picture it. "The thing is, though, is that they were made of skin, y'know? There's some Inuks out there that make art like that. They take a caribou hide, get it real wet, and put it on a wooden mask and let it dry and the mask will keep its shape." The uncle peeked through his fingers.

"They cut out the eyes and the mouth and sew fur around them to make 'em look real. The ones in Igali's room though, they creeped me out." The uncle sat closer to his nephew. His voice hushed. "I was just about to run away when I heard something, eh? Something like—like crying. Like a sob or, or weeping in another room, y'know? I leaned in closer and then—"

The kitchen door crashed open. The uncle and nephew both yelled, startled. Behind an armful of groceries, the boy's mother stood in the doorway.

"Little help?" she uttered as the uncle and nephew steadied their breaths. They rushed to the mother and went to work putting the groceries away. After a moment the mother ran a hand through her hair.

"So, what were you two yelling about?" The mother looked back

36 | Jamesie Fournier

and forth between her brother and her child. "You screamed like you'd seen a ghost." The uncle and the boy exchanged a look.

"Unc was telling me scary stories!" the boy replied excitedly. His uncle winced at the words and avoided his sister's gaze. She groaned as she filled her pantry with cans of soup.

The uncle cleared his throat as a grin flashed across his face. "Halloween's coming up, y'know? Gotta get the boy in the spirit! I'm still taking him out trick-or-treating, right?" The worry in the man's voice was palpable.

The mother sucked her teeth and exhaled. "As long as it's just stories. No. Horror. Movies." She tapped each word with a bundle of carrots against her brother's heavy chest. "He's too young. He gets nightmares, and where is cool *Unc* going to be then, huh?"

"Well, I'd hate to break it to you, Sis, but I think that ship's sailed." The uncle uttered under his breath. The mother turned to her son who stood sheepishly behind. The uncle spread out his arms. "Well, we watched horror movies when we were young and we turned out fine." The uncle tried to clear the air.

The mother turned back to the cupboard. "Ughh, don't remind me," she groaned as she stocked the pantry. "I still think about the one about that witch that drank that kid's blood or whatever."

"Oh!" the uncle exclaimed excitedly. "No, it was a warlock that needed the fat of an unbaptized child!" The uncle laughed as he recalled the movie. He sighed, lost in memory. "It was awesome." His sister turned and gave her brother an accusing look. Her worried gaze shifted from her brother to her son and back again. The uncle turned to the boy. "What? You were baptised, right?" The uncle waved his hand. "Bah, you're fine." His sister lobbed a pack of pasta at her brother. The man expertly caught the pack.

Mask & Bone | 37

"Y'see that, neph? Reflexes like an eagle, this one!" He curled a bicep, spaghetti in hand.

The mother gently closed the pantry and walked to her son and kissed him on the forehead. "So, if you two weirdos are okay for a bit longer, I'm going to go get cleaned up." She raised her eyebrows and looked her son and brother in the eyes. Her brother put his hands in his pockets and smiled. Her son filed in beside the uncle and did the same. She rolled her eyes and then started up the stairs. The boy turned to his uncle who gazed into the pack of spaghetti.

"Y'know," the uncle said, "in Hansel and Gretel, they never tell you why she was after those kids. The witch, I mean. There was food everywhere, right? You know what I think?" The boy nodded as his uncle crouched. "Think about it. Young kids believe in magic, eh? They believe in spirits and other worlds and ancient beings and all that." The uncle's eyes were wide. "Now, say if you could *absorb* that energy, that life force. In Inuktitut, we call it *inua*. And say you can take that belief, that fear, that inua—that would feed a creature whose entire existence relies upon belief. Upon fear. A witch in the woods." The uncle looked to his nephew and pointed a finger. "The amautaliit in the Wastes. When people stop believing, when people stop being afraid, those creatures can fade away into nothing. So, they change. They evolve. They make a house out of candy. They adapt or die."

The boy's face stilled; his Adam's apple bobbed. The uncle continued, "So, this witch figures it wouldn't take much, just a couple kids every few years or so. Enough to get by, enough to feel . . ." The uncle paused, trying to find the right word. He then snapped his fingers and slowly lowered his gaze. "Re-ju-venated."

His gruff voiced purred over every syllable.

"Is-is that what they did?" The nephew's young voice quavered. "The amautaliit, I mean." He looked silently at his uncle, unsure. The man looked the small boy up and down and debated whether or not to continue. The uncle straightened his back and looked outside the kitchen window. Sunlight streaked in from the setting sun, cascaded through the glass, and scattered across the man's cold gaze. He tightened his lips, exhaled, and looked down to his feet. He absently kicked a bannock crumb across the floor.

"Well, y'know how I told you about my friend that went missing?"

"Eric?" The small boy nodded.

"Yeah, that's him." The uncle smacked his lips. "Well, that day at Igali's, when I saw those damned masks. It was so quiet I could hear my own heartbeat. And Igali's room started to fill with shadows. But there was something else, like a soft crying not too far away. Just on the other side of the dark, y'know? Like an echo." The boy watched as his uncle shifted uneasily. "And I looked at those masks . . . " The man's voice cracked as he wiped his eyes. "And I knew what I heard. I knew. I could see it. The mask, it looked like it was sleeping but it was sad, too. Sad sleeping. But the fur, the fur, that—that sealed the deal." The uncle dragged a sleeve across his nose. His lips drew into a sneer.

"I knew it was Eric. It was his parka. It was his fur. And the more I looked at that damned mask, the more I could hear him crying in the back of my mind. And then. Then your mom found me staring at the damned mask. She only heard her baby brother crying, so she came to help, but when she came in, she stared into those faces and heard it, too. Children! Crying! Their faces frozen. She kept 'em like trophies, y'see? Igali!"

The boy's eyes shimmered, unable to turn away from his uncle. "W-what happened? When mom found you?" he managed to whisper.

"Igali came in and found us. Your mom and I just standing there. Crying, staring at that blasted wall. And Igali—she just stood there." The man's voice pitched sharply. "We turned to her, and she looked so cold. She wasn't the aunty we knew. Slowly, she knelt and looked us dead in the eye as we stood just sobbing. Just a couple of kids, eh? Just kids wanting our aunty to help us. But she wouldn't! She just stared! But then, slowly, slowly she brought a finger to her lips, shushed, and then turned her head side to side." The man swallowed and looked at the floor. He held his head in between his knees before he looked back up to his nephew. "I'll never forget that look. She then took us by our hands and led us out to the kitchen and made us stand by the stove.

"*'You may not understand,* qiturngaak. *But this is what we do. This is what we have to do to survive,*' she growled, calling them the Inuktitut word for 'children' as she pointed to her large stone cooking pot over the stove. Stew bubbled and boiled. The coppery scent of meat cooking permeated everything. We looked up and saw small, gleaming bones in the sauce. '*We take their inua and we move on,*' she said. '*Their faces bind them to me. Nothing goes to waste. None of them. They are all a part of me.*' She nodded to our empty bowls, licked her lips, and smiled. '*As they are a part of you.*'"

The uncle held his nephew's eyes intently. The boy began to cough. "Your mom and I started bawling all over again." The uncle's voice wavered. "We could still hear all those damned kids, crying all at the same time in those . . . masks. Igali. She held us by our shoulders, her voice like wind ripping through trees."

"'The world needs their monsters,' she said. 'Without fear they are proud. Without fear they do not appreciate life. This is who we are. There are no more children in the Wastes! Our world needs balance. And now, now you will help maintain that balance—my niece. My nephew. This is your inheritance.' Igali held us steady with her glare. 'This is your birthright.'

"She then reached into her pot and slowly pulled out a bone covered in meat. It was small. Tiny. And once it came out, we knew what it was." The uncle's voice choked. "It was a leg." The man sobbed. "A b-baby's leg." He wept. "And, as it came out, Igali sank her teeth into it and pulled. A long, thin piece peeled right off. She then c-cut it with her *ulu* and stuffed the rest into her mouth. She licked her fingers and walked away, leaving your mom and I alone staring at the damn stew, knowing what it was." The boy's stomach twisted as his uncle's face turned deep red.

"And then something changed . . . inside. We grew hungry. Reallll hungry." The uncle purred, angry and full of tears. "I poured myself a bowl and I chewed and I savoured and I felt that sweeeeet flesh melt against my tongue. Your mom," the uncle whispered, "your mom didn't even use a bowl. She just started to shovel handfuls into her mouth. We were in a frenzy! Both of us chewing and swallowing, knowing full well what it was. Fat swirled down my throat and coursed through my veins sending jolts of black electricity surging through my body. Marrow dribbled down my chin and I felt . . . alive!" The uncle roared as the nephew squirmed out of his chair. The man's voice trembled terribly. "The earth crawled beneath my feet. I could feel the stones and the dirt and the rocks. I could feel every insect in the cosmos. Volcanoes of energy erupted all about me," he growled. "The universe grinded on its own horrible axis and it was me and I was it!" The uncle turned to his nephew, his eyes filled with hatred. His voice like ground thunder. **"I. Was. Rejuvenated."**

The boy fell to the floor. His body convulsed, unable to voice what rolled through him. He turned his gaze and his eyes widened. Igali's long stone pot bubbled above him on the stove. The boy began to hyperventilate. Shocked, he looked down to his hands. Roots of pain pulsed out of his fingertips and into the world. Hot iron bubbled in his mouth as a dark vein of the universe split open and greeted him into anti-life.

"Don't fight it, kid." His uncle crouched down, placing a hand on his shoulder. "You'll give yourself brain bubbles." The boy's breath shuddered as his heart stilled. The black mortar between worlds yawned. "I'm sorry, Ajak. It's better this way. It's better that you know." His uncle righted the chair and eased him back into his seat. He patted his shoulder and wiped gravy from his lips. "You won't have to do it often, little Ajak. Just when ya need to." His uncle pointed. "Don't get greedy. Keep moving. Always keep moving," his uncle recited as he snapped his fingers, lost in the rules written long ago. "You gotta follow the food, hm?" The boy turned his head and stared coldly. The uncle chuckled, "I mean, if you wanna live forever, you gotta keep a low profile. Be on the watch." The uncle stopped and looked at his nephew with genuine care.

The mother came down the stairs in her pyjamas. She ruffled a towel through her wet hair. She stopped at the final step and looked to her brother. Her brother stared back and nodded only once. She inhaled slowly then paced over to her son. She held his head close to her chest. "Oh, hunny, you're freezing!" She pushed back her son and held his head in her hands. "Have some more stew, it'll warm you up." She turned and poured another steaming bowl. Cubes of soft, tender meat dropped from the ladle. She turned and smiled at her son; her canines flashed briefly. She handed her son the bowl and then went and flicked on the radio. A tinny voice crackled from the speakers.

"*—years old, wearing tan shorts, red t-shirt, and a blue baseball cap. The boy's parents are pleading for his safe return. The boy was last seen . . .*"

The mother rose, turned the radio back off, and returned to her seat. "Ugh, the world can be so awful sometimes."

"You can say that again," the uncle stated as he slowly stood in the small kitchen. He looked down to the small boy, what was left of him, and knew that a part of his young nephew had died that day, deep down inside. But something else had been born. Something much more ancient. The man reached to the counter, grabbed the boy's cap, and pulled it over his nephew's head. The man smiled, put on his own hat, and walked out the door. His nephew sat in shocked silence. He peeled off the hat and looked it over. His fingertips ran over the embroidered blue bird. The hat turned in his hands. It shimmered and bristled as if it were a thing alive. Yet, in the back of the boy's mind, he swore he heard the faint whimper of a sobbing child echo, as if it were just on the other side of the dark.

Taima

I Am Enough

Rachel and Sean Qitsualik-Tinsley

Excerpt: From the Journal of Iphigenia Twold
August 13, 1967

He was a boisterous Frenchman who loved to talk. While my trip up from the south had been cozy, one might even say comfortable, Xavier's little plane alarmed me, even as the man himself went on as if he were the happiest of party drunks. The vehicle rattled like a canister filled with a thousand invisible bolts, sounding ready to fly apart and let me plunge into icy waters. Or the tundra. I was never sure of which we flew over from hour to hour. But amidst the noise was Xavier's constant, casual hollering about "single-engines" and "high wings" and "propeller-driven STOLs." Sometimes, his voice was a reassuring distraction. At other times, I valued his rare silences, as I wanted to take in what little I could see of the dun hills or dark tides below us.

I had done my research and was eager to arrive and try out my meagre language skills, being even more keen to behold the environment for myself. But one does not truly appreciate a treeless landscape until it plays out before the eyes. People from deserts might, I suppose. And I had long read that this Arctic environ, geologically, qualified as a desert, albeit a frigid one. As I flew, I wondered if anything could grow here. Even flowers.

Now, I have landed and can continue my journaling for the sake of professionalism, rather than self-reflection: a Social Worker in my first Arctic community. I suddenly wish that my eyes were cameras, so that everyone I know could see this place as I do. There are indeed flowers here. Poppies! Small and delicate and of light gold, as if the sun on the water had somehow continued up past the pebbly shore and been captured in the form of bobbing clusters. There are more grisly things, too, albeit fascinating: the heads and flippers of walruses left beside overturned dogsleds that have only recently been put aside with the passing of snows, as summer is so short in this place. I spotted some dogs; lean, wiry huskies of tan and white fur, wandering along the distant curves of beach. No people, yet. But I admit to some impatience, and I am scrawling away as if in a fever. I hope that I can interpret my own handwriting while reviewing these notes in years to come! Xavier is almost finished unloading the plane and I should write more tonight.

From the Journal of Iphigenia Twold
August 13, 1967

"I should write more tonight." That is how I naively ended my last entry. But it turns out that there is no "tonight." I write this just before bed, yet the sun is still in the sky. The cabin set aside for me, a dingy shack really, had some enormous wool blankets left by someone before me. I have layered a couple over the only window, blocking out the light. Luckily, there are quite a few spare tools, and I hope no future occupants mind some nail holes along the edges of the blankets.

I did not think I would mind the iron stove, but now that I am here, I somehow dislike the look of it. The thing squats like a great black mushroom edged with rust, taking up more space than I would have liked. The cabin is cramped enough as it is, though perhaps that is a plus. It will force me out more often to connect with the people. Perhaps even to become a member of this community. Thanks to Dad, I know how to use the stove, and there is a lot of wood. Xavier made a gallant show of inspecting the kindling pile outside, to see if there was enough for me, though I do have eyes of my own.

I have placed Dad's Norelco "carry-corder" on the desk next to me while I write this. A proud gift to his Social Worker daughter. He alone was supportive of my switch away from English Literature. From my earliest memories, even when I brought two poor, dying, doomed blue jays home for "surgery," he understood my passion to help the disadvantaged. And I think I will put the recording gadget to healthy use in interviews. I still believe that I packed far too much bulk and weight in cassettes and batteries, and am already beginning to wonder if, in the isolation, books would have been better. But reading might have eroded my focus. I need no distractions from my good work here. And the recorder at least reminds me of family.

The village is surprising. Lonely. I have seen little of it, in my sheer exhaustion upon arriving and setting up a bit, though I did spot a few of the pathetically simple "matchbox" houses while hauling bags from shore to shack. I have heard of such structures. The government graciously built them as a reward to those Eskimos who agreed to abandon their benighted lifestyle, which, difficult as it is to conceive, apparently used to sprawl amid the entire wilderness. The word "barren" is used as early as the writings of Knud Rasmussen in describing the Arctic, and I am arriving in what I understand to be a far more enlightened era. Yet it is impossible to imagine how anyone might eke out the merest of lifestyles, much less healthy existences, while relying upon so little. In catching even a glimpse of this housing, I am sure that the Government of the Northwest Territories could do more in providing for these people, though, as Dad reminded me, I must take care to outwardly establish myself with my employers by cultivating a loyal demeanor. Though I will only write it for the sake of this journal, the housing situation in this community unsettles me. To call these buildings squalid might constitute a compliment. Though I am not yet familiar enough with this place to know whether or not I am entirely looking at housing, or simple shacks for storage, the condition of my own cabin suggests the former. I am looking forward to inspecting the village and conferring with fellow professionals, pursuant to writing up eventual recommendations for improvements.

(Including removal of those unsanitary walrus parts along the beach.)

Oddly, none of the Eskimos I am here to serve have come out to greet me. Do they know who I am, or why I am here? Nor was I met by any RCMP officers, as I had expected. I am not sure how to orient myself in this place and will have to rely most heavily upon the briefings I received before departing from Frobisher Bay. I hate to ask Xavier, for even the most casual of questions sets him on a ranting spiral of adventurous exposition, but I was to meet a native here by the name of Jayko. Perhaps it would be better to connect with other Whites first, though. The local doctor? Minister? Priest? When I see Xavier off tomorrow, I will remember to ask where I can find educated people.

I feel strangely unwell. A combination of nerves and fatigue, with thoughts flocking like birds. More tomorrow.

From the Journal of Iphigenia Twold
August 14, 1967

Sleep was traitorous at best. The oil paint swirls that substituted for dreams included a churn of images from the last few days. Rancid walrus heads roared at me with thick French accents. My cabin buzzed over ice and water, ever approaching but never arriving at some looming, fungal structure.

I awoke, however, to the most lovely of days, albeit one of mixed content. Today, with the sun poised like a fresh gold dollar in the blue, Xavier and Jayko met me down by the beach. Apparently, the men have some past with each other, though, with all his talk, I do not know why the Frenchman had not mentioned it before. The two are almost like a comic team, quick to tease and laugh at or with one another. Yet I would mark Jayko almost as Xavier's opposite, being a small man, lean and even a bit frail in appearance, with an almost clerical bearing. Though Eskimo, he is not as Asiatic in appearance as I would have expected, and he reminds me more of some foreign worker of mixed heritage. Like Xavier, Jayko is perhaps in his late 30s. When still, I could not help but visualize him as made of driftwood, like some improvised children's toy. And yet, as he lifted cargo to hand to his departing friend, I could see sinews writhe like wrestling worms under the bronze skin of his forearms.

Though accented in such a way that his "s" is more like a "sh" in sound, Jayko's English is excellent. Like the few Eskimos I have met in Frobisher Bay, he tends to pronounce each syllable with great care, as if it were a word unto itself. He seemed to ignore my own attempt at the native greeting of "kan-wee-peet," leaving me privately embarrassed, for I may have mispronounced the word. After greeting me with a gentle handshake, Jayko proceeded to explain to me that, after Xavier's departure, I will be the only Causasian remaining in town. I must admit to some alarm at hearing this, and it must have shown on my face. He smiled kindly, however, assuring me that many adults in the village know at least a bit of English, while a few even know some French (a fact that I suppose pleases Xavier). But I was disappointed to hear that all semblances of civilization are invested elsewhere, accessible by boat in the summer and dog team the rest of the year. Doctors, for example, have not visited for two years, and health matters, including even the delivery of children, are left to local means that I imagine can only resemble the medieval.

Missionaries, apparently, have come and gone. There was a small church back before Jayko was born, and upon this point Xavier and Jayko at first agreed. They fell to squabbling, however, when it came to exactly who burned the structure down. Xavier insisted that the church was Roman Catholic, put to the torch by jealous Anglicans, while Jayko claimed exactly the opposite. I listened patiently, not confessing to my relief that there were no religious figures now present. Among the dossiers that I reviewed, I saw too much inclusion of religious opinion as it is, and I do not believe that superstitious matters should conflict with mandates of state. The state alone is the one hope for the humane and egalitarian, and we need no more churches. Spiritual inclusion, of course, is reflective of outdated policies that I can only debate with my superiors once I rise in rank and influence.

I was less pleased to hear that there are no police, and that the nearest outpost of RCMP are expected to respond to criminal matters by visiting the community for the sake of "significant criminal investigations." Though I remind myself that the Eskimos are often described as a gentle people, how will I, as a Social Worker, be able to enforce my judgements? How do I intervene, for instance, in a case of child abuse, especially amongst a population inured to the violence of hunting? To carrying rifles?

I mentioned this to Jayko and Xavier. They simply looked at each other and laughed. I asked why.

"There's no store, either," said Jayko. "People bring in supplies from other communities."

"That means bullets are precious," added Xavier. "Nobody's going to waste one on you."

It was a strain to smile along with them.

From the Journal of Iphigenia Twold
August 17, 1967

... and I said as much to Jayko. To his credit, he seemed to sympathize with my point of view. But he cautioned that, while patient with Whites, it is a local custom for families not to interfere in each other's business. I suppose, in that regard, I am deemed a "family" of one. The notion that I am an oddity without kindred, here, is perhaps supported by the fact that, soon after our mild locking of horns, Jayko asked me if I had a husband. I told him that there were no husbands in my foreseeable future, and that was that. It might be supposed that this was my first truly questionable experience in this place, as it did leave me fuming for some time. Yet I must strive to remember that these are, through no fault of their own, uncultured folk, and a lack of civility is to be expected so distant from populated centres.

Nevertheless, the girls Jayko introduced me to are marvellous. They are a pair of cousins, apparently, named May and Sheela. I was puzzled as to why, when I inquired past their broken English what ages they were, both shrugged and loosed a giggle. To me, they seem about eleven or twelve years of age, though apparently one does not necessarily keep track of one's age in this village. It is just one of the many peculiar customs, such as those I documented only yesterday, but not confined, apparently, to this village alone. Jayko seems to have intuited that I need constant advising, and he speaks as though he were adopting a tone of general apology for what he senses must be a dizzying array of quirks and behaviours herein, whether in language or custom.

Like the rest of the villagers I have thus far met, including Jayko, May and Sheela do not seem as Asiatic in appearance as I had expected from old photographs of Eskimo people. They are indeed quite tan, almost to the point of seeming burnished, and slim limbs are often juxtaposed to heavier frames in torso and face. Yet there is no consistent look here, nor racial profile that I might use for comparison, for even the relatives of the girls vary, some of their own frames being small and short, attached to long and heavy arms. Other than dark eyes, the only feature that I find consistent from native to native seems to be hair. At first, perhaps due to seeing it fleetingly or in shadow, I assumed their hair to be raven in the way common to the Eskimo people. It was when I saw it flash in the sun that I realized that it is in fact red, albeit so dark that it resembles congealed blood. Except among the quite aged, whose hair seems smoky in colouration, the locks of young and old, even of the aforementioned cousins, features at least one streak of white. Thus far, Jayko is the only villager I have met who seems free of this peculiarity.

Other features, I am sad to report, include deformity. While the unaesthetic and exceptional to nature occur in every culture, I have encountered such with unusual frequency among these villagers. Much is luckily subtle, so that many individuals Jayko introduced me to displayed only ungainly strides or asymmetrical posture. I spotted two, however, in the house of May and Sheela, with more severe conditions, making me sorely miss a medical professional with whom I could consult. It is tragic that the government seems oblivious to the individual concerns of these people, and they shall certainly hear of such in my dedicated reports. Fortunately, the reputed care for their disabled, for which Arctic peoples are renowned, does apply here. Sheela's mother (May's aunt), while I only gained glimpses of her, seems to occupy her own room. From her back room, perhaps a bedroom, she appears to be a figure of some esteem, ill concealing a deformed leg, restless and clearly pained, with a decorative blanket, while members of the family (I assume) bring what Jayko reports to be delicacies of fresh organ meat. On the other hand, Sheela herself, as with her cousin May, appears to be in good cheer and free of all blemish. This is a happy observation for me, as children concern me most of all.

As the young cousins were all smiles and bubbly laughter, quite welcoming and seemingly fascinated by this pale stranger, the adults around them were the opposite. I am not sure whether they were at all pleased at Jayko bringing me to their little house, which was only in slightly better repair than my own shack. Their smiles, as they hurried back and forth, inside and out again, were fleeting at best. Nor was I ever greeted by the adults with more than a cursory nod, as if they regretted acknowledging my presence. Still, I am not ready to label them rude. After all, I am the oddity in this place, and I would be a fool to think that one more government worker would earn instant trust. I realize that it is not until the natives see me as a fellow human being, and in turn realize that I acknowledge them as the same, that I may be deemed a proper "ee-ka-yook-tee" (the local word for a "helper").

Indeed, the smiles eventually dropped even from the faces of May and Sheela after some minutes, as though they had either grown bored of me or finished with some allotted time that they had budgeted for greeting a stranger. I must admit to some concern at the transition, and I wondered if I had offended them by saying something gauche. But they muttered to Jayko in their language, varying between the glottal and sibilant, that they must check on the "puppies." Perhaps unwilling to yet release them from what had been a jovial, even welcoming, moment, I tried to overturn the now sombre atmosphere by stating that I love puppies (indeed, I do!) and would appreciate seeing them. Instead, May wrinkled her nose in an unmistakable expression of distaste, while Sheela whispered furtively. The two then wheeled about to make for the back door, leaving me to ask Jayko for a translation of Sheela's words.

"She said the puppies are not for you," he told me. At once, he looked concerned, and I sensed that there was something amiss in this situation. Jayko assured me that all would be well and that it is not the local custom to dwell upon such things, as White people do. It was only once outside, in the blessed sunshine and fresh air, that I assured Jayko that the social situation in this place truly is my concern. Families and their dynamics are, after all, the very reason why I am here. I further assured him that I do understand my own awkwardness, and that I intend to learn the customs of the Eskimos so that I may be the best "helper" that I can be.

He wrinkled his nose, saying, "These people are not Eskimos."

From the Journal of Iphigenia Twold
August 20, 1967

... just as I have not been able to forget Jayko's peculiar statement. Not Eskimos? Despite my attempt to dismiss these words, I finally found them recurring in dreams. Horrific dreams, in which poppies rained blood into my own hair, whereupon it ran in streaks that turned to white.

I have not forfeited my entire library in coming here, having retained three books that I felt might disentangle the peculiarities of Arctic cultures. I brought only those that discussed language, however academically and abstrusely, as well as the histories of some explorers. I recall Mother suggesting that I bring some works concerning legend and religion, but I deem such subjects to be useless relative to even the greatest of the world's cultures. I was pleased, at first, upon reviewing some features of language, believing that I had unlocked the reason for Jayko's cryptic statement from days past. In retrospect, I do not know why I did not simply ask him what he had meant. Perhaps I am trying too hard to prove that I can master this place. Even that I belong here?

Whatever the case, I approached Jayko with the bearing of some pitiful student who had at last solved a master's riddle. I gushed out something like, "Now I know why you said these people aren't Eskimos." Trying out a new word, I added, "That's because they call themselves *Ee-noo-eet*."

Jayko stared at me for a moment, then smiled, his dark eyes at once admixing pity with the grin.

"No," he told me. "They aren't Inuit." (I will substitute "i" and "u" herein, rather than the linguist's "ee," and "oo," in order to reflect Jayko's pronunciation.)

That was when Jayko gestured me away from the buildings, down toward the beach, as though what he next told me risked overhearing. By whom, I do not know. Once he was content in his distance from the village, he explained to me that he was only half-local, and that his mother had been a woman from one of the distant Inuit communities. I reverted, at once, to the term of Eskimo, insisting that the government recognized all the Eskimos of this region as being of the same ethnicity. This area, I insisted, had been well mapped and thoroughly explored, with somewhat esteemed ethnologists having come and gone for some time. Yet Jayko, in that stubborn way I have already become accustomed to, insisted that the Queen's people (as he termed the government) are newcomers to the Arctic. Inuit, he added to my surprise, are similarly newcomers, yet they have been here long enough to know more than the Whites: such knowledge, apparently, including the fact that there were other peoples here even before Eskimos.

I must confess to some confusion in listening to his pseudo-history of the Arctic, which may be characteristic of the superstition that prevails in this part of the world. Jayko nevertheless seemed ardent in insisting that, when true Eskimos moved into this part of the Arctic, they had a great deal to teach some of the peoples who were already here. Other peoples, if I understood him correctly, had already found "ancient" means to live here—knowledge that some Eskimo groups adopted in turn. I admit that I am a bit fascinated by this phenomenon of myth-making, with its fantastical explanations of migrations, intermingling of peoples, and even supposed extinctions. I must have seemed a bit obtuse to poor Jayko, as we spoke to the point where I earned myself a sunburn, and I was still only able to inculcate those bits of narrative that he seemed bent on repeating. The sum of it all, if I gather it correctly, appears to be that the turn of centuries eventually saw newer people usurping previous cultures, those who had survived in "ways" distasteful to the now-dominant Eskimos. Inuit, Jayko insisted, were now the common people of the Arctic.

But not here.

From the Journal of Iphigenia Twold
August 26, 1967

I went to see May's family today. Normally, it is the custom among these people to simply walk into a home without so much as a knock. Yet Jayko seemed odd and brooding, not at all his usual jovial self, and insisted that I wait outside while he called past the front door, asking if it was acceptable for us to enter.

May, as it turned out, was present, yet her mood was no better than Jayko's, and I began to wonder if there had been some death in the village.

(Note: How are the deceased handled? With the general lack of educated individuals in the community, I find it unlikely that there is a proper undertaker.)

May had trouble looking me in the eye, and in the awkward silence, which these people do not seem to mind, I felt compelled to ask how Sheela was doing. I was told that she had come down with an illness and was resting at home. I then asked how the puppies were doing, reiterating my desire to see them.

In English, May responded, "They are all dead."

I was taken aback, so much that even I could not think of anything to combat the next discomfiting silence, and simply stared at the floor until, perhaps bored or insulted by my questioning, May walked past me and left the home. Jayko then informed me that we should go. Perhaps realizing that I was a bit shaken, he afterward took me on a walk to continue showing me the community. We walked past broken and abandoned tools, gnarled driftwood that children had brought up from the shore, and the occasional skeleton of an Arctic char. I was finally comforted by the sight of reedy little sandpipers picking at invisible bugs, while ghostlike snow geese nibbled amongst the waving sedge between beach and village. All the while, I wanted to express to Jayko how jarred I was by the constant juxtaposition of joy and death in this place, but I knew how weak I would sound.

I was distracted by a sight in the distance: that of a small hill, or whatever some geographer might call it, standing out by the fact that all else had seemed rather flat up until then, as well as by the fact that its top seemed flat. Now that I recall it in my mind's eye, I suppose another odd feature of the hill was that it was sandy, as if a great clot of beach had defiantly risen to stand in the distance, so that it was quite unlike the rocky, sedgy environs characterizing the rest of the village. Some patches along its sides further seemed yellow in colouration, and I now wonder if this was sunlight or clusters of the yellow poppies so common in this area. At the point at which I noted it, Jayko and I stood almost on the opposite side of town, and I asked him what was over there.

"That's for those who have passed over," he told me. I asked him if, by that, he meant a cemetery, but he simply chuckled. I doubt that I will ever become accustomed to the inordinate way in which these people frame the simplest of things.

Now that the day is done and I yawn over this page, I realize that, had I questioned Jayko concerning the strangeness with May, the ostensible sickness with Sheela, I would not have known what to properly ask. I think that I was disturbed by the silences, the mood changes, the purported fate of the puppies, because I am sensing a deeper meaning behind it all. I know that I have formed a sort of bond with the two cousins. Though we three barely know each other, I cannot evade the feeling that I am somehow here for them. For their welfare. Perhaps it is simply that the alienness of this village, the sheer culture shock, is spurring wild fantasy. Perhaps it is only that I want so badly to uplift amid the general erosion of human dignity that I see in this place. But I must acknowledge some hope that the girls feel the same way about me: that they understand, on some level, that my mission is for them. I wonder if they are unconsciously trying to signal, to me, their need for help. Children, it is understood, speak in allegory: stating truths through their body language and the regulation of their emotions. Is Sheela indeed "sick"? Are the puppies "dead"? Is it possible that May was trying to hint at something?

Perhaps there is a reason why the adults have not welcomed me. As a Social Worker, I may have my first cases.

From the Journal of Iphigenia Twold
August 29, 1967

I have realized that I must be careful not to alienate Jayko. Since our confrontation yesterday, he has been noticeably colder, though I also wonder if he broods over the religious concerns that had sparked our argument in the first place. Though not wholly one of these villagers, he is a complex man and no easier to comprehend than one who has lived his entire life herein. I might have been more respectful, I suppose, though his talk about consulting with his "ancestors" and "helpers" and an ill-defined concept called the "Hee-la" admittedly raised my temper, reminding me of Christian clerical hubris admixed with Eastern mysticism. For a moment, I thought of indulging him, for his perspective is one with which he was raised. But then he babbled something like, "We need to watch. For the special day. The Passing Over."

This Abrahamic reference, clearly meant to refer to Passover, proved to me that I am not simply dealing with native religion, but rather a ridiculous, hybridized belief system that has no place in the rational world. I will not tolerate compromise of my good work for the sake of local taboo admixed with remnants of missionary zeal. It is exactly because of such spiritual and cultural misdirection that May and Sheela are not receiving the care that the average child deserves. And if it is to any degree my duty to listen to Jayko's explanations for the progressive deterioration of these children, then it is at least his counter-duty to acknowledge my authority as their case worker. Still, I cannot afford to lose Jayko as an assistant, since my ability to communicate with May and Sheela in their time of need would be severely hampered.

I have visited the girls' respective houses several times now, and the adults are little warmer to me than before, which increases the feeling that there is a social dynamic in which I am not to interfere. This in turn, of course, makes me suspect that it is a negative dynamic, which, along with the depressed condition of the children, has me wondering about abuse. Only Sheela's mother, whenever she spots me from her back room, greets me with a smile and a wave. Her name, apparently, is Nipee (as with most names, I must assign a spelling herein), and I sense that I must somehow gain private access to her in order to discuss the girls. I do not know, however, how lucid the woman is, as she seems quite unwell. Nipee is so grey and bloated, limbs shifting in obvious pain beneath her sprawling blanket, that under any other circumstances I would have expected her to be Sheela's grandmother. Sheela's father, conversely, seems like a much younger man, glowering at me from under a heavy brow as he ranges back and forth, in and out of the house, pausing only to step into the room with his wife, whereupon he slams the door.

I thought about interviewing the general family despite Jayko's protestations, though I now wonder if this would be going too far, too fast. Jayko has volunteered his time thus far, and he is not a government employee. I cannot compel him to work with me. But neither can I abandon the girls, who seem weaker and more despondent each time that I meet them. Jayko insists that his perspective is proven because of the puppies, as well as the "terrible day" (a reference I have heard several times now, without explanation), but am I to let superstitious responses to rumour and random happening keep me from my duty? Even if I were the coldest of hearts and utterly without pity for these suffering children, I do not suppose that my superiors would smile at reports of how I failed in my mandate out of ostensible respect for community gossip or Jayko's supernatural beliefs. As I noted yesterday, I like neither the slouching, shuffling affect of these now-ashen girls, nor the desolate look that ought to be alien to any child's gaze. Were there sickness present among the adults, even in myself after visitation, I might dismiss such observations. Instead, as my indulgence of this culture continues, I increasingly feel that I am asked to advocate more for abuse than for Sheela and May.

I should force myself into bed, though I have begun to look at the sheets with distaste. Exhausted as I am, I have lost any desire for sleep. Lying down is simply an exercise in pressing my eyes shut, only to have thoughts of the children scrape like broken pottery along the insides of my cranium. In those rare hours when sleep does come, I am harassed by a sense of what I can only term beckoning, as if I were slowly realizing that I was supposed to have reached some ill-defined point, now missed, where sound (yet, something that is not quite sound?) is somehow more significant than sight. When I experience this sort of dream, I awake with my own nails digging into one of my limbs. I worry that I will wake, one of these times, to see that I have drawn red. I do not know how

I could be so emotionally weak, and this nauseates me. I have no right to be so brittle in the face of the children's needs.

I have some candy. What would Jayko think of me investigating from my cabin?

Transcript of Recorded Interview
Social Worker Iphigenia Twold w. Sheela Kitiktook and May Oosee
(Jayko Tayarnak Interpreting)
Excerpt Recovered by Sgt. Bradley Dunn, R.C.M.P., G Division
September 05, 1967

Iphigenia: Make yourselves comfortable. Sorry it isn't a bit bigger! May, you can have that stool over there, if you please. The stove is still hot. Jayko, you can be our microphone man.

[Laughter. Indistinct words.]

Iphigenia: You'll just have to split the last candy between you. Or ... May, that's very kind of you, giving it to Sheela. Well, first of all, I wanted to thank you both for this interview. And thank you, Jayko, for agreeing to translate.

Jayko: I should do a prayer, first.

[Long silence.]

Iphigenia: Well, I suppose a short prayer would be alright.

Jayko: [speaks in guttural sounds; indistinct words.]

Sheela: [Speaks in Eskimo.]

[Long silence.]

Iphigenia: Is everything alright?

Jayko: She says it doesn't like it.

Iphigenia: I'm ... afraid I don't understand.

Jayko: My prayer. It doesn't like it. She says so. She says, if I keep praying, they're not allowed to talk.

[Long silence.]

Iphigenia: I don't really understand what's going on. But Sheela, May, anything you need to make you comfortable, okay?

Jayko: You should stop this. It wants them to talk to you. You should stop it.

Iphigenia: About what?

May [in Eskimo]: The terrible day.

Jayko: You should stop. Something's wrong.

Iphigenia: May, I'd very much like to hear about the terrible day. Everything else on your mind, as well. Sheela, you too.

May [Esk.]: It won't make sense unless you know about the flowers.

Sheela [Esk.]: That's where we found them.

Iphigenia: Found what?

May [Esk.]: The caterpillars.

Sheela [Esk.]: They were beautiful. Furry. Like tiny puppies.

May [Esk.]: But we thought they were dead at first. They were icy. Frozen. With the flowers.

Sheela [Esk.]: When we took them home, they thawed out and started moving. That was when we knew they were hungry. There were three of them. They fit right in my palm. But they couldn't tell us what to feed them.

May [Esk.]: But there was the dog.

Sheela [Esk.]: Yes, the mother dog. It had just had puppies, and they were nursing. She had plenty of milk. So, we gave them over to the mother dog.

May [Esk.]: We knew they were thirsty. We somehow knew.

Sheela [Esk.]: They made us know.

[Long silence.]

Iphigenia: May, listen carefully. You too, Sheela. Are you really . . . talking about something else? Something you're afraid to say out loud?

Sheela [Esk.]: We're not really telling you. It's Ma'ha. It wants you to know.

Jayko: They're telling the truth.

Iphigenia: Jayko, please. Very well, let's keep talking about the "caterpillars." May, Sheela, did your parents know about these caterpillars? Anyone else but yourselves?

[Long silence.]

Iphigenia: I wish there were more candy. How about some tea? Look, I'm very honoured that you're talking to me. That you're entrusting me with this. Please, go on. I really do want to hear.

May [Esk.]: We just couldn't understand, at first. What they wanted.

Iphigenia: Your family?

May [Esk.]: The caterpillars. Their voices were too curled. Round and round.

Sheela [Esk.]: And we had to hear with sight. That was painful. But you could hear them inside your eyes.

May [Esk.]: And behind your eyes. As sounds that were curled.

Sheela [Esk.]: Maybe that's why the milk wasn't enough. It wasn't curled enough. Neither were the puppies themselves.

Iphigenia: I don't understand. Curled? Are you translating that right, Jayko?

Sheela [Esk.]: Not enough. The puppies.

May [Esk.]: Or the mother dog.

Sheela [Esk.]: When we went back a couple days later, a couple of caterpillars had starved. We hadn't been close enough to hear them crying out to us. Because the puppies and their mother weren't enough. But one caterpillar survived. We thought it would die, too, because it was weak. It could barely put thoughts in our eyes.

May [Esk.]: But then there was Ma'ha.

Sheela [Esk.]: It came like wind, but not one that makes you cold. That's how we knew. Ma'ha placed stronger sounds in our eyes. We could even smell them. And they didn't curl. They went straight in, so we knew where to put the caterpillars.

Jayko: You should end this.

I Am Enough | 67

Iphigenia: Jayko, please. Go on, May. Sheela. I'm . . . interested to hear. Whatever you might say.

May [Esk.]: We carried the caterpillar, and we were the home it wanted.

Sheela [Esk.]: Right here. I had it at first. Then May.

Iphigenia: Your leg. I don't understand.

Sheela [Esk.]: You see the duffel socks? Very high. Lots of room. And warm.

May [Esk.]: Behind the knee was its favourite. We didn't like putting it there at first. It touches, makes your skin feel like you do when you can't tell if you're asleep or awake. And it puts light that isn't behind your eyes. But it makes sure you don't mind after a while. It makes you dream, even in the day.

Sheela [Esk.]: When it got bigger, it came up to the thigh. Because it needed more. We couldn't sleep because it was always making sounds. Not the noise of light, behind the eyes. It was, "*Tee-tee-tee. . . .*" But we didn't really need sleep because we dreamed all the time. Even walking around.

May [Esk.]: Sometimes, it would forget to make us dream. Then there was pain. So much that we couldn't remember who we were. Where we were. Feeling it on the leg, but not just there. Also, in the deep inside, where we keep our names. All we could think of, then, was stopping everything, just to get away. But that would get its attention again. Then, we weren't sure if we were feeling it. We smelled it, tasted it, saw through eyes that were not eyes, but all at once. That was confusing.

Sheela [Esk.]: But it was a good husband. It didn't want us to feel pain. It didn't want us confused.

Iphigenia: Excuse me? Is that word correct? Husband?

Jayko: That's what they call it.

Sheela [Esk.]: We knew it would need more one day. But it was a good husband, then. It just wanted the curled parts of us. The red space.

[Long silence.]

Iphigenia: I'm sorry. Jayko, I'm not . . . sure what this all means. Red space?

Jayko: They mean blood.

Iphigenia: May, Sheela, focus for me, please. Tell me about the terrible day.

Jayko: You should stop this.

Sheela [Esk.]: It grew so fast. Such soft fur. But not like an animal's.

After a while, it could leave on its own. Make its way around while everyone slept.

May [Esk.]: But that's how the dogs found it.

Sheela [Esk.]: We felt the wounds behind our eyes. Smelled screams.

May [shouting]: *TEE! TEE! TEE! TEE! TEE!*

[Long silence. Chairs shuffling.]

Sheela [Esk.]: When we got outside, we saw the pack of dogs. They had blood all over them. Walking in circles around it.

May [Esk.]: Near the beach.

Sheela [Esk.]: Our husband. It looked like torn up rags.

May [Esk.]: Or a baby.

[Sounds of weeping.]

Iphigenia: I don't have any tissue, but here. Wipe on this.

Jayko: I won't do this anymore.

[Chair scraping.]

[Long silence.]

[Transcript ends.]

From the Journal of Iphigenia Twold
September 07, 1967

As I feared, Jayko is avoiding me. He is far more profoundly affected by the contents of the interview than I would have suspected, though I myself am shaken for different reasons. Unlike Jayko, who seems convinced that May and Sheela willingly offered their blood to something unwholesome, and that all such madness is overarched by a Ma'ha (which may be a concept or name, I am not sure which), I am instead disturbed by the metaphors at play here. "Husbands" that are caterpillars? Confused sensations? Themes of violation? I do not believe that I must be Doctors Freud or Jung to imagine what these might connote. Jayko could be of great service to me right now, but in crossing paths with him yesterday, he would not look me in the eye, muttering only that he must "prepare" himself. Perhaps unsurprisingly, he then evaded my questioning by diverting to talk of Ma'ha and how it was still "present." I admit that I grew terse with impatience, for I will not subscribe to his belief that the health of the girls hinges on some form of ritual.

I believe that it is at least possible to harvest a second interview from Sheela and May, as they seemed willing to talk before Jayko's walk-off. But I must persist at winning back Jayko, for he is the only way to gather a reliable translation. Perhaps I should indulge him, if for no other reason than to glean his full, however skewed, perspective on the matter?

Despite my exhaustion, I cannot fail these innocent girls, who are clearly suffering under the abuse of as-yet-undisclosed family members. I will not stand by while the light in their eyes diminishes by the day, while their childish effervescence is drained to that same grey inertia afflicting every part of the adult world in this era. I will not let the squalor of their environment become a squalor, rather, of the soul.

Yet at least it appears that, in exhaustion, there is a distinct peak. I have tired myself to the point where sleep comes easily now, and my dreams have given way to the pleasant. They are my only respite from what is becoming a steadily more nightmarish reality.

From the Journal of Iphigenia Twold
September 08, 1967

The sun no longer circles the horizon in the level way of the Arctic's eternal summer, but now dips lower and lower, so that sometimes I cannot see it, other than its glow from behind distant hills. Chill winds raise great whitecaps out at sea, and flocks of birds fly here and there, as if unsure of where to land at any given time. In the frigid morning, I found that many poppies outside my cabin had frozen. If this is the coming of winter, as Xavier and Jayko had forewarned weeks ago, then it does not come stealing in with a gentle turn of seasons, as I am accustomed to in my own homeland, but rather as a brute conqueror. Strange that the cold did not wake me, though. My dreams have seemed abyssally deep of late, and imagery that now seems lurid to recall was accompanied, in slumber, by only the most pleasant of sensations. The last images I recall include a single hole in my leg. I think that it did not cause me physical pain, but rather wounded me in some newly discovered part of myself, probing something at once within and without, like winding ribbons of life of which I had never been previously aware. I was then approached by a rust-coloured dog, clearly missing ears and eyes, yet wagging its tail in a manner that filled me with a most powerful sense of welcome. It licked at my wound, and I could feel the saliva entering therein, at once healing and imparting a sense of delicious fulfillment. For a moment, I had the sense of something enwombed. Not in me, but in the Earth itself, as if the very planet were a great, blessed apple, playing host for the most holy of worms.

[Illegible section.]

Just now, I almost tore out this page, but I will simply refocus. Something came over me while describing my aforementioned dreams, a savage, selfish impulse unworthy of a servant of the people. I have no fatigue to blame, this time, and I can only speculate that this place is testing my character. It is a test that I am more than adequate to pass.

I cornered Jayko today, seeing him from afar and near the elevated graveyard. Though I nearly burst my lungs in running after him, he finally stopped for me. I almost regretted seeing him. While uncombed hair and dishevelled clothes are not unusual for the men of this village, his eyes were wild and bloodshot. He further seemed, somehow, to have lost some weight, for he was lean as one of the pieces of driftwood along the shore. He further wore a leather thong around his head, so thin and tight that it dug into the flesh of his forehead. Around one fist and its corresponding wrist, he had wound a kind of ribbon or belt, from which dangled tiny, yellowed figurines. I assumed these to be of walrus ivory or antler, which

I knew the natives put to myriad uses. Yet everything I had seen carved from such substances had thus far been practical, for use as or with tools of the hunt. These figures instead seemed only to be of animals, including what might have been a wolf or dog, a bird of some sort, and perhaps a bear. There was also a tiny effigy of a knife, its subtle greenish tint hinting at antler, the sight of which seemed to lock my gaze in ill-understood fascination, until Jayko asked me what I wanted.

Awkwardly, I tried to issue pleasantries, which I hoped to receive in kind, though Jayko would have none of it. So, I told him of my intent to interview May and Sheela several more times, perhaps even their families, all the while emphasizing that I needed him for perfect translation. He chuffed dismissively, telling me that I was in danger because I had "listened" (whatever that meant). He then went on about the caterpillars again, assuring me that his previous rituals had failed, that no good could come from dwelling on May and Sheela, and that since they had been "tasted," they were bound to wither away to the "place only Ma'ha knows." I must confess that this drew red rage from me, as I understandably objected to the notion that superstition must reign in the fate of girls who so clearly cannot voice their own suffering beyond the use of fantastic themes and nightmarish metaphor. I said as much, adding that it was shameful for Jayko to abandon these girls in such a way. He grew angry at me in turn, adding that he was already haggard from the many "songs of his mother" he had sung against the "wedding feast." He then devolved into his general, mad drivel concerning nebulous helpers, Ma'ha, visions, fasts, ancestors, and family connections, claiming that he had to somehow use what he termed the Great Breath, or Hee-la, to clean away those that "ride in on the light that is not light."

Coming uncomfortably close to me, so that I could see the dirt in his pores, smell the sourness of his breath, he told me, "I'm scared. I don't know if Inuit ways will work here. I'll use what my mother taught me, though. In three days, I go to fight."

I could then see the fear in his gaze, alternating with glimpses of determination. Or perhaps I had finally come to eye incarnate madness. We stood for a long while like that, assessing each other, while his figurines clacked against each other like dull chimes. Without another word, he turned and marched away, leaving me alone in the increasingly chill wind.

From the Journal of Iphigenia Twold
September 10, 1967

Dad's recorder is gone. It was an easy matter to overturn everything in the cabin. I have never taken it outside, so I know that I couldn't have left it anywhere. But what really leaves no doubt of theft is that the cassettes and batteries are also missing. I know that it was Jayko. He alone knew that I was intent on continuing with more interviews of May and Sheela. It seems that he has found a way to most emphatically manifest his hitherto strenuous objections. Perhaps I have a part to play in this. I should not have pushed him so when his mood was so intemperate.

I still have paper, though. That might be enough. Nothing will keep me away from the girls. They occupy most of my dreams now, along with the light that pushes me.

Nothing.

[The bottom half of this page is burned away.]

From the Journal of Iphigenia Twold
September 11, 1967

I awoke to what I thought was singing. But it was not joyous. As I cracked the door to the cabin, wind sweeping at papers until I feared they might be sucked out to flutter down the beach, I could hear distant howls, alternating with animalistic guttural sounds that seemed to blend into frantic chants. Then silence reigned, sudden as a gunshot. I listened some more, hearing only wind and what might have been dogs.

I write this in a backward fashion, having shut the door and returned not to bed, but rather my desk. It appears that I fell asleep after a most arduous day. My feet still ache. Up and down, I walked through the community today, searching for May and Sheela. Indeed, any word of them at all. No one would speak to me, and the affected smiles have all evaporated. I struggle, now, not to hate these folk, and not to hate the conflict that has manifested between my dreams and waking life. It seems as if I now walk the halls of nightmare, while blissful dreams, filled with quickened light and sounds that impart the richest of scents, play at some whirling space within me. Were it not for my concern over the girls, I would welcome sleep over anything of rancid reality.

[There is a section of the journal, here, that is illegible due to fire damage.]

I have discovered an envelope, crudely sealed with rumpled edges. I have no idea where it was originally placed, though with no lock on my cabin door, anyone can place anything with as much ease as when my Norelco was taken. I opened the door just now, though, so the wind must have swept about the cabin, carrying the envelope out to where I could readily see it.

The letter inside is yellowed, soiled with dark marks, and there is clear evidence of old graphite having been rubbed out over and over, so that the paper could be reused. It simply reads:

YOUR MACHINE IS AT SHEELA'S HOUSE. MEET TOMORROW. JAYKO

I feel triumphant. Though I am nevertheless angered by the original theft, it seems that some droplet of goodwill still exists between myself and others in this community. I have no idea how to interpret the prospective return of the recorder. It might be voluntary on the part of Jayko, though I can no longer speculate on his poor, mercurial mind. It is conceivable that he came around in perspective, or at least realized that the mature decision is to echo my own past attempts at showing respect. But then, perhaps this has nothing to do with Jayko himself. Could it be that May and Sheela are pressuring him to continue with the interviews?

My steel is again with me. Tomorrow, I will be a proper servant of the people. I will go to the house and meet Jayko, perhaps to renew our work together. If I am fortunate, Sheela, maybe even May, will also be there. And I will demand answers from any family that are present. For the sake of my remaining sanity. For the sake of the good work that I have thus far done.

For the sake of the girls.

Transcript
Social Worker Iphigenia Twold
(w. Possible Voice of Nipee Kitiktook and Unknown Male)
Recording Recovered by Sgt. Bradley Dunn, R.C.M.P., G Division
[1967?]

Iphigenia: Thank you for having me here, Nipee, though I was expecting Jayko. It's a nice back room you have. Very colourful.

[Indistinct words, possibly from unknown male.]

Iphigenia: No, thank you. I've already had a lot of tea today. I'm here for business, I'm afraid. Nipee, I would really like to know where Sheela is. Or May. Did you just ... click on ... is that my recorder?

Nipee: Yes, it will be useful. For remembering.

[Long silence.]

Iphigenia: Your English is ... surprisingly good, Nipee. Jayko should have told me that. Well, thank you for the return of my machine. Do ... you happen to know where the extra cassettes and batteries are?

Nipee: It will be for teaching. Thanks for it.

[Sound of footsteps. Indistinct male voice.]

Iphigenia: I'm trying to be patient, but this is becoming ridiculous. That's my recorder and I demand its return. My father gave it to me.

Nipee: We are your family.

[Long silence.]

Iphigenia: I'm flattered. But I didn't give that recorder to anyone. It was taken from my cabin. Did Jayko give it to you? Is he here?

Nipee: He's here.

Iphigenia: In the house?

Nipee: In here.

Iphigenia: Well, I want to speak to him, please. I'm trying to be polite, but I believe I'm owed an explanation for what's going on.

[Indistinct male voice.]

Iphigenia: Well, I disagree. I am a government representative, and I intend to file due reports to my superiors, who should be expecting them soon. I assure you, they'll include my suspicions concerning Sheela and May, so I recommend cooperation. If you want to clarify events, I would be happy to include anything you have to contribute.

[Indistinct male voice.]

Iphigenia: Jayko sent me a letter requesting that I meet him here. But my primary concerns are still Sheela and May.

Nipee: We sent you the letter. It was the best way. For the first time, we'll record the Passing Over.

Iphigenia: You . . . sent that? I demand to see Sheela. May.

Nipee: No one can see them anymore. They were not enough. It's like that sometimes. Not enough.

[Long silence.]

Iphigenia: What the hell are you talking about?

[Sounds of possible wood paneling and/or door slamming.]

Iphigenia: Open that at once!

[Sound of boots on floorboards.]

Nipee: I will miss my daughter. My niece. But we miss all of them. Always. Like other women of my family, before me. Sometimes, they are tasted. But sometimes, they are not enough. But we always have to try. That's what Ma'ha says.

Iphigenia: Jayko's "Ma'ha . . ."

Nipee: Not Jayko's. He was never really one of us. Much like his mother. Inuit always hated Ma'ha. But they don't really know because they're newcomers. Ma'ha was here long before there were people.

[Indistinct male voice.]

Iphigenia: What do you mean, "here when the stars were different"? What does that even mean?

Nipee: Even when there is no one here to recognize the new stars, Ma'ha will be here. That's why Ma'ha asks us to place the caterpillars. Where the children can find them. So they can drink. Then eat. Then sing to the curled light between the stars. But it is up to Ma'ha whether the caterpillars grow.

Iphigenia: More of this . . . won't subscribe to this. Can't . . . I must be misunderstanding.

Nipee: We know because of Ma'ha, who met with the first of our family. And Ma'ha gave husbands to our women, who offered their legs. All are tasted. But not all taste of a proper wife. So not all keep a husband.

Iphigenia: Jayko. I need Jayko. He can make sense of this maybe . . .

Nipee [laughing]: He is here.

Iphigenia: Where? May I speak to him, please?

Nipee: You can speak, but he doesn't understand anyone. Not anymore. [Laughter.] I have a lot of blankets.

[Shuffling sounds.]

[Choked noise, possibly from Iphigenia.]

Iphigenia: That's not Jayko! Is that . . .

[Laughter from Nipee and unknown male.]

Iphigenia: What happened to his arms? That's his face, isn't it? His body ...

Nipee: He can no longer hear with words. But he will be blessed with being present for the Passing Over.

[Sound of chair scraping, possibly falling over.]

Iphigenia: This is sick. I have to go. I have to ...

Nipee: My husbands are old now. I am the best of my family's women, but I am no longer enough.

[Sounds of a possible struggle.]

Iphigenia: No!

Nipee [laughing]: Come closer. See my husbands. It has always taken a big blanket to keep both of them warm.

[Female scream, possibly Iphigenia.]

Nipee: They have not drunk for a long time.

[Sounds of struggle.]

Nipee: Only eaten.

Iphigenia [voice suddenly close to microphone]: TO ANYONE WHO RECOVERS THIS! THEY AREN'T LEGS! THEY AREN'T LEGS!

[Dull thudding noise.]

Nipee: I am no longer enough.

[Transcript ends due to unidentified, high-pitched sounds, followed by irreparable tape damage.]

Taaliqtuq

Malcolm Kempt

I POINT MY RIFLE AT THE RABBIT AND THEN I AM THE RABBIT staring back at myself when the bullet strikes me *akuliaq* before I have a chance to run away but then I am myself again unable to shake the feeling of the strange encounter so that when I collect its lifeless body from the tundra I find myself unsettled by the whole experience which forces me to ponder my own death as I stare at the carcass of the *ukaliq* to wonder if the bullet also ended my life and when I trudge out across the frozen ocean toward my community I walk backward to avoid taking my eyes off the place where I might have died and in doing so find myself lost for several days without food or water but unable to bring myself to eat the ukaliq who has become my travelling companion and whispers to me of all the things he has seen and done in his short life upon the land and when we lie down on an *ujarak* to rest together after what feels like years of endless walking I dream of an unkindness of ravens scattered black against the whiteness of the freshly fallen snow while collecting tattered feathers in their beaks outside the *iglu* where I last laid in the arms of my beloved mother as a helpless infant before she was consumed by that fire in her brain so many years ago and in this twisted vision slowly bleeding through the fabric of my mind her long hair constricts around me like the black cocoon of a *tarralikisaaq* and as our bodies meld together into one flesh one creature with one heart who for one moment held a precious breath and then let it go to watch it crystallize in the cold night air before it drifted up *taaqtumi* between the stars where no one ever travels and when I die in this melancholic reverie I do not wake but sink down deeper into the depths of the harbour beneath the churning waves where the grieving sun can never find me where my body drifts face down across the bottom of the ocean with my crippled hands dragging in the thick silt of the seabed where the furrows they create fill with starving crabs that follow my aimless wandering in hopes to gorge upon my flesh should my corpse ever come to rest but then there is a moment oh so brief in this fleeting dream when I am floating up toward the surface and break free like a fish trying to catch a fly that is flitting too close to the water and in doing so he enters the world above him for an instant before he splashes back down into a darkness that he only knows as home while trying to hold on to who he was while he was up there and to remember all he said and did while he was soaring through the air but it slips so quickly from his memory like the windswept snow between the crosses of the graveyard near my home and when I finally awaken from this nightmare within a dream I find myself buried barely alive beneath the stones of a burial mound with my rotted *atigi* wrapped around me and my rusted gun and *pana* laid beside me while the rabbit comes and goes from a narrow space between the rocks to bring me snow that he melts between his bloodied paws and rubs across my frost-burnt lips to slake my thirst and keep my hopes alive with tales of *nungusuittuq* and although I am exhausted I still watch the maggots as they writhe within my wounds to devour my whole body as it is in this life but shall not be in the next and in the end I do indeed die and my *tarniq* slips out across the surface of the ice like the wind keeping pace with hunters on their snowmobiles as they race across the bay in search of caribou at night while my *atiq* drifts back toward the distant lights that I call home to find a newborn to call its own and the desperate creature deep within me gnaws at my intestines until it claws its way up through my yellowed teeth to voice its yearning for the things that made my life worth living which are now nowhere to be seen since it is *taaqsivalliajuq* as I stand alone out there on the snowy beach beneath the cliffs where the seabirds used to come to nest and there I open the fuel container and let the fumes burn my nostrils and throat and eyes as I douse myself to start a fire to keep me warm in this winter that never ends where the air is so thick with frost and then there is the sudden smell of burning hair and flesh and the screams of all those I have wronged and there is only pain in every inch of me as I inhale the heat and ash and smoke before the melting and the cracking of the frozen lake beneath my feet sends shivers through my immolated bones until the ice finally gives way and I am consumed not by the frigid water underfoot but by the laments and regrets hardening like cement within my arteries and the everlasting cold that penetrates my ears my eyes my nose my mouth until I am frozen to death and no longer feel the warmth of life that I once knew as a child when I would kneel to butcher seals that I had shot at the *agluit* out on the sea ice and I still taste the salt water on my tongue as I hold its viscera up to see it steaming in the light of the waning moon and then look down to see my own guts spilling out over my naked thighs and know that the seal and you and I are all the same in blood in bone in breath and we are not far from one another in life or in our deaths and I remember that there is only one father and one mother who guide and welcome us back into the fold when all is said and done and when I stop cutting myself just for a moment to look down at what I have done I realize that the spiders have awoken from their hibernation among the mosses that my blood is now feeding and they crawl up my legs until I am fully covered in their blackness and I look to be a shadow of my former self and then I hear the gunshots echo out across the once-silent landscape of the snow to know that the *tuktu* finally are all dead and gone and we have lost this silent secret war with ourselves that we never knew we were fighting and then I collapse upon the tundra in a crumpled heap of sobbing and become my son and then myself again and then my father and his father and his father and his father all the way back to the very beginning whenever that may be and when I finally wander home through the afterlife to see the buildings of my community that remind me of old headstones lined in rows along the shoreline I shuffle up the well-worn path that leads me through the hummocks into the town of my birth toward my house where my wife greets me like a stranger but still invites me inside where I witness my reflection in our bathroom *tarraqtuut* and I understand her reluctance because the person looking back is not the man I once was or the man my *aippaq* hoped that I would be and so I rush out of the building in a rage of self-loathing narrowly avoiding the gaping jaws of the dog lunging and snarling to test the strength of its ice-encrusted chain with its bone-white teeth snapping inches from my frightened face and the warm spittle from its blackened lips spattering on my cheeks and when I reach the jagged edge of town where light becomes night my legs burn with the sulphuric acid in my veins and the damned mosquitoes are so thick I cannot scream without inhaling them until my lungs are full with all their tiny cadavers and I tell myself that there is beauty in this desolation and peace in my isolation and purpose in my suffering but in truth I am so lonely and cold and tired that I let myself slip into that long-awaited darkness beneath the darkness like a man into a warm bath of his own flesh and blood and then find myself alone again *ukaliqsiuqtunga* out on the tundra where I point my rifle at the rabbit and then I am the rabbit staring back at myself when the bullet strikes me akuliaq before I have a chance to run away

Watch It!
Gayle Uyagaqi Kabloona

Susi slowly blinked her eyes open and grimaced at the horsefly-sized drone-cam hovering above her. The first hint of dawn filtered through the flapping red fabric of the tent. Her older sister, Annga, was already outside boiling water for breakfast. Susi stretched her sore legs inside her corporation-issue sleeping bag and groaned, dreading the day ahead.

Susi and Annga, teenage sisters, had experienced heavy rain throughout the competition, or "experience," as they were supposed to refer to it. Yet miraculously, they'd remained one of the top contenders. Susi knew their success so far was thanks to Annga. Annga was the one who handled the updates and maps, decided the best routes, found the food caches, and pushed them physically and mentally. They received periodical updates on the n/fo-pod strapped to Annga's wrist, issued to them along with the rest of their gear from the corporation.

Susi didn't bother with the updates or learning how to read the maps on the n/fo-pod; she trusted her older sister to take care of those things. Annga was possessive of the tech anyway. Susi just strapped on her pack and followed Annga across the difficult Arctic terrain. Really, she wondered why she was chosen to take part in this thing in the first place. She just felt like dead weight lugged along the rocky tundra.

The American media megacorporation Anomale was the biggest television distributor in the world. American media was one of the last economies that had held up over the decades since the last world war. They broadcast in every major language from their glowing satellite ring around the planet. Anomale was particularly popular for their reality TV series. This was one of their survival-style races that pitted teams against each other in the last remaining wild areas of the world. Five billion subscribers had accounts to watch live feeds of their favourite teams' progress.

In a plot twist this season, every team was Indigenous. Susi and Annga were the Inuit team. To make the prize more enticing to a new pool of "applicants," Anomale announced that the winners would receive humanitarian aid for their communities. The prize would be doled out as years of guaranteed food, medicine, energy expenditures, technology advancements, and scholarships. The added group responsibility was supposed to make for a better race.

"Applicants" became "contenders" entirely without their knowledge. Anomale used cookies to choose people based on whatever internal guidelines they operated under. Susi and Annga didn't know why they were chosen, but they certainly hadn't applied. Nevertheless, they were bound by responsibility to participate on the slim chance they'd come out in first place. The sisters certainly felt the added stress on top of the already difficult situation. They dreaded letting down their family and extended community; there were too many futures riding on their performance.

"Get up, *nukaq*, you have to eat before we get the update. I want to be packed and out of here the second it comes in," Annga said through the tent fabric.

"Ughhh," muttered Susi. She was so warm inside the fluffy bag. They were given equipment and supplies she'd never dreamed of before. Lightweight, quick-drying clothes, puffy sleep systems, and calorie-dense dehydrated food. She sat up, still wrapped in her sleeping bag, and reached for her outdoor clothes. They had dried nicely overnight.

Susi unzipped the door and stepped out onto the gravel where they'd pitched their tent. She was met by more drone-cams positioned to capture every angle. "Jesus, they could have made these things stealthier, they're so fuckin' annoying," Susi complained as she waved one away from her face. "They're like *kitturiat*."

"Don't swat at them!" Annga made a move to grab Susi's arms. "You literally signed papers saying you wouldn't wreck corporation property! And besides, the whole point of this thing is to broadcast it."

"I didn't ask to be doing this," Susi hissed at her sister, attempting to find an angle where the vids couldn't read her lips.

"Goddammit, Susi!" Annga stood up from where she'd been crouching over the butane stove. "Shut it! At least pretend! We have a once-in-a-lifetime opportunity here and the whole freaking community is relying on us. Stop being selfish."

"Oh, fuck off, you really think we could win this? The whole thing is rigged. We were chosen to fail for ratings."

"You don't know that. We've gotten this far. And we're competing on our own land. None of the other groups have that advantage."

"Yeah, yeah, whatever. . . ." Susi muttered. "I'll be the *hero we need!*" she said sarcastically and made a face at the nearest drone-cam. She walked off dramatically to find a rock and pretend she had privacy.

By the time she returned, trailed by a cloud of blinking drones, Annga had torn down the tent and packed it. A bowl of rehydrated oatmeal with berries sat steaming, waiting for her.

"Thanks for being ready by the time I asked you to. . . ." Annga glared at her little sister accusingly. "Anyway, the update came in. We're heading southwest along the Owl River until we hit the Rundle River, and then we'll head toward Mount Battle and the glaciers up that way."

"Yeah, yeah. I'll be ready to go in a second," Susi said unenthusiastically. "I just can't wait to start today's slog!" She made a rock-and-roll sign with her fingers as she sat on the ground to scarf down her oatmeal. The drones settled into a resting formation around her head.

Susi and Annga came from a large family for the time: five siblings, Annga being the oldest. Their parents had scrimped and saved to send Annga to a prestigious boarding school in the South for a good education. They were banking on Annga getting one of the few lucrative jobs left nowadays, to come home and support the family. Susi was resentful of the attention and praise her parents gave Annga. Annga only came home once a year now, but she constantly talked a big talk about her bright future.

Annga was always good at assuming whatever role people wanted her to take. She could reflect anyone's version of how they wanted her to be, easily code switching between their world and the outside. Annga didn't look like the rest of the family. She was white-passing, with light brown, wavy hair, big, deep-set eyes, long limbs, and light skin; her nose even became red in the cold. Susi, on the other hand, turned out looking like her Inuit mother and aunties; she had small hands and feet, full, high cheeks, her eyes nearly closed when she laughed, and she wore her sleek, dark hair in braids.

Susi secretly thought Annga was a traitor and craved attention. She might seem like the perfect envoy from the North, but Susi doubted her sister would return home once she graduated. She once overheard Annga tell a friend that she went by her middle name, Madeleine, while at school. Susi wondered if Annga would make the most of the reality show fame to boost her social capital and online presence. She wished others could see through Annga's favourite-child facade and see who she really was—narcissistic and two-faced.

To begin "the experience," the sisters were brought to Pangnirtung Fiord, at the north side entrance of Akshayuk Pass, by mega-drone. This was approximately one hundred kilometres south of the community of Qikiqtarjuaq in the olden days. It had once been a part of Auyuittuq National Park. Akshayuk Pass was a highly regarded hundred-kilometre wilderness trek for experienced backpackers, climbers, and adventurers in the 1900s and early 2000s. Climate change and overuse had forced the park to close in 2031. Nowadays, only the uber rich could afford to fly . . . and a washed-out glacier pass full of rocks was probably not at the top of their destination list.

Neither Annga nor Susi had been into the pass before. They grew up in a camp north of Qikiqtarjuaq, but they'd never had occasion to go so far into glacier country before. They had lived a mostly subsistence lifestyle, fishing, hunting, and harvesting on the land and water. The area covered in ice caps or glacier runoff didn't support any prey animals, so was pretty useless for them to go into. The pass was a novel landscape for them.

Huge glaciers had carved the immense blocks of dark grey rock into peaks, cliffs, and steep ravines. When the sun shone, meltwater from some of the last remaining glaciers on Earth poured off the tops of the mountains in noisy waterfalls. Scree interspersed with monstrous boulders had been deposited by much larger historic glaciers and created moraines at every valley. The sisters' path so far had led them from the north-facing fiord southward to the centre of a peninsula. At first, they hiked over soft tundra made of green, tan, and brown mosses and lichens, small flowers, and low-growing plants. Gradually the plant life gave way to loose rock and gravel as they moved up the river valley toward the centre of the peninsula. There, the last of the glaciers all converged and tossed the landscape into a jumble of rock and ice. The drainage patterns changed with every season's freeze and thaw cycle, and the amount of meltwater and rainfall.

The sisters hadn't seen a single other team for the entire time they'd been out on this "experience." They got rankings on their n/fo-pods, but no other information. They were left to wonder if they would encounter opposing teams at some kind of orchestrated confrontation. They'd seen some of Anomale's programming and didn't put it past the corporation to put them in a dangerous situation—*a fight to the finish*. They crossed their fingers against that possibility, since they weren't physically formidable in any way. Annga was the taller of the two, towering two inches over Susi at 5'4." Plus, Susi was scrawny from limited resources in their home community. The odds were against them; they were a true underdog story.

The sisters continued to trek uphill as the day wore on. What began as fog and drizzle in the morning became a full-on downpour by the afternoon. The hummocky tundra they traversed became a knee-deep watery bog. They plodded along the eastern side of the Owl River, a broad, silty expanse that meandered in braids in low-lying areas. The tops of the 2,500-metre-high mountains next to them were hidden by thick mist. The girls heard deep, booming cracks from above as boulders loosened in the rushing rain and meltwater and fell from their clinging perches. The sisters skirted around the older boulder fields, hoping they were out of reach of the falling debris.

What were trickles of slow-moving runoff during the previous days became crashing torrents. Rainwater swelled and broke over the edges of the runoff grooves, icy water racing to converge with the broad, clouded river in the centre of the pass's valley.

Even their high-tech gear couldn't stand up to the amount of wet that poured down. Their fingers were pruned inside their gloves, their feet sloshed inside their boots, and water seeped in through the seams of their garments. Their packs seemed to double in weight as everything became soaked and retained water. Even the drone-cams sagged in the air, looking tired and wet in solidarity. The girls blinked solemnly as they struggled against the fat water droplets.

Susi took deep, heaving breaths as they climbed over slippery, moss-covered boulders and attempted to circumvent swollen ponds. "I hate rain, and I'm in pain. Hating pain, in rain ... raining paiiiinnn *ai ja ja ja ja....*" she sang morosely. Her legs throbbed from days of overexertion and her lungs burned; what small amount of stamina she had was being tested to the limit.

They hadn't seen any wildlife since they'd started trekking, not even a bird. Susi had lots of birds for their precious viewers though. She flipped the nearest drone the bird she was most fond of. She was averaging about ten of those a day. She hoped the producers were making a stupid compilation of them.

She was staring down at the terrain, finding safe notches in boulders and flat areas to place her feet. She paused on a large rock at the crest of the incline they were ascending and looked up for her sister. She couldn't see her amid the dark, wet rocks, relentless rain, and stifling fog.

"Annga?" she called. She squinted and strained her neck to look up and over the nearest boulders, but couldn't spot her. She looked around and back from where they'd come and saw nothing. "Shit," she muttered. She carefully stepped down from the rock she was on to search for her sister.

Shit, shit, shit, she thought. Suddenly, the grey day seemed not just dark, but ominous. The fog suddenly hid unknown dangers and adversaries—bears and terrifying surprises sent by the corporation. She strained her ears to listen for movement and heard nothing. Just the sound of rain falling and pebbles cracking downhill in the rushing waters.

Susi struggled uphill, more tense than before. When she stepped between two large boulders, she nearly jumped out of her skin. Annga was crouched down behind one of them, hidden from her view.

"Jesus Christ, Annga! What are you doing? You nearly scared me to death." Susi clutched her chest, adrenalin coursing through her veins.

"Relax, we just got an update on the n/fo-pod. I'm trying to hide from the rain."

"How's that working for you?" Susi asked tersely. "It's not raining sideways . . . yet."

But she was relieved to have found Annga. Those few brief

moments alone were enough to give her the chills. No matter how annoyed she got with her sister, she didn't want to be abandoned out here. The environment was harsh enough, but she had a nagging fear at the back of her mind that the corporation was planning something nefarious that would manifest soon.

"Jeez, I thought the corp . . ." she muttered, more to herself, ". . . took you away or something. . . ."

"*Huva?*" her sister said as she looked up from the n/fo-pod.

"Nothing," Susi said. "And since when are you speaking Inuktitut again?" She put her hand on her hip and gave her sister an accusatory look. Of course, Annga would play it up for the cameras. *Sure, you're super Inuk now that you're on TV*, she thought, annoyed. "What's the update say?"

Annga shut her eyes and took a deep breath "Whatever, Susi. The update just wants us to do a personal vlog. Say how the experience is going and stuff."

Susi scoffed. "You're serious?" She looked up at the bleak day, felt the cold water running down her back inside her jacket, and rolled her eyes. "Mmm-k."

"I know how you feel, but try not to be a super bitch about it, okay? This is an opportunity, not a prison sentence."

"I mean, kinda feels worse than prison if I'm being honest," Susi answered. "If we were in prison we'd be inside and wouldn't be busting our asses climbing this mountain."

"Uh-huh, just tell it to your drones, not me, okay?" Annga told her. "And go somewhere else, I'm doing mine here."

"Ugh." Susi turned and walked for a few minutes to be out of earshot. She sat down on her pack facing the valley. Maybe it would have been pretty if she wasn't freezing cold and the weather was astronomically different. Maybe if they could at least see the view. . . . Or if there were any animals at all, any sign of life. It was like the caribou and polar bears had abandoned them. They knew better than to be in this creepy mountain valley.

She took a deep breath and sighed. She put her face down in her hands, trying to think of something to say. Her drone-cams hovered at their preferred angles, waiting patiently. Susi wondered about the subscribers viewing her at home. How warm and dry they must be. How they'd probably be cooking or doing chores with her on in the background, just a distraction from their mundane daily lives.

"I don't know . . ." she started. She looked at the drone in front of her, lost for words for once. "I . . . I never wanted to be here. I never wanted to be on TV. Is that why I'm here? Is that why I was picked?" The hovering drones gave her no answer, just continued to record.

"I get Annga being chosen, but why me? I just . . ." Susi took a big, heaving sigh. "I wish I was home. I don't care that we don't have much. I don't want to leave like Annga, I've never wanted to. The world seems so big, and I don't want a part in it. It can go on without me. Leave me in my little camp with the same people I grew up with. I'll live the little life. Just fish and forage every day, and sometimes I don't even need to see anyone or say anything. I hate the idea of people knowing me from this. I don't want to be known. I just want to go home and be small. Not be a rat in a maze, struggling for the entertainment of strangers who don't know my way of life.

"*Taima*," Susi said finally. She had some more thoughts, but she refused to divulge everything to the drones and the invisible audience.

She walked back to her sister. Annga had finished her vlog and already boiled water on the stove for lunch. Rehydrated Caribbean rice and beans awaited Susi. "Oh, good. I'm starving," she said as she sat down next to her sister.

"The next update says to keep heading toward Battle Mountain. We'll have to cross the Rundle River in order to get there," said Annga.

"Okay," Susi mumbled as she devoured her meal.

Annga was organizing her pack, already working out next steps. But she had a strange look on her face, more withdrawn than usual, beaten down.

"What's up with you?" asked Susi.

Annga's eyes darted to her sister. "Nothing," she said. "I'm fine."

"Weird, 'cause you look not fine," said Susi, squinting suspiciously at her.

"How I look isn't any of your business," she answered, exasperated.

"'Kay, you don't have to be like that. I was just asking." Susi was annoyed that she'd even tried talking to Annga.

The mountains above them were emitting deep rumblings and cracks at a higher occurrence than before. Annga packed up their things and took off. She was headed toward the swollen glacial river flowing ahead. Susi moped after her.

A small drone, bigger than their drone-cams, appeared and hovered in her way. It was carrying a small package. Curious, Susi extended her hand. The drone dropped it, then swooped toward the mountain and disappeared. Annga was too far ahead to have noticed. Susi looked inside the package and pulled out a small n/fo-pod, the same kind as the one Annga wore.

What the . . . ? Susi wondered. She looked at the small screen and read the message illuminated there. YOU ARE THE LAST PAIR IN

Watch It! | 101

THE COMPETITION, it read. *Oh my god*, thought Susi, *we must have won!*

The screen blinked a new message. THIS SEASON THERE CAN ONLY BE ONE WINNER.

Susi stood dumbfounded. *What the hell does that mean?* she thought. She looked up the mountainside at her sister's retreating form.

GET RID OF YOUR SISTER, the n/fo-pod blinked.

Susi stood completely still. She stared at the screen. "You can't be serious," she whispered to it. She looked up at her drone-cams, and they seemed to move closer. The n/fo-pod blinked again, the same message, GET RID OF YOUR SISTER.

She stayed rooted in place. She couldn't wrap her head around what the message said. *Get rid of her . . . like how?* She thought of the past seasons of the show. This had never happened before. Each season a pair or team won. Scenes of ecstatic winners flashed in her mind's eye. The sisters had been forced to compete in this thing against their wills, but Susi always had her sister by her side, no matter if they were arguing or how much she drove her crazy. Annga was always there for Susi . . . there was no way she was going to *get rid of her sister*.

This was the last straw. She had been pushed to her limits already, jumped through hoops for this damn show, made to feel like a spectacle inside a fishbowl for the stupid subscribers. No, fuck this show, fuck this place, she was done. She realized she was still holding onto the newly delivered n/fo-pod. She turned around and threw the pod down the hill into the rocks. "Go to hell!" she screamed. She attempted to snatch the drone-cams out of the air around her. They were capturing all the best angles of this new development, but they flew just out of her reach.

She stopped trying to annihilate the drones as her mind caught up with her. She realized that Annga must have gotten this message too. Could her sister actually be considering getting rid of her? Her heart dropped. *Fuck, that's why Annga had looked weird when I returned from doing my vlog*, she thought.

She had barely had this realization before a huge boom echoed from above. They had come closer to the glacier's toe but still hadn't been able to see it through the fog. Deep, echoing cracks and booms sounded one after the other. The sound of rushing water reached her ears. She looked up toward her sister, who had stopped her ascent to listen as well.

The blood drained from Susi's face. She was frozen in place, but knew she had to move quickly. They were too close to the river. Water must have pooled inside a natural rock dam inside the mountain cirque where the multiple glaciers drained. The rain had been so intense that the weight and force of the trapped water broke through the natural deposited rock dam. The sound of smashing rock and crashing water became louder.

A two-metre-high tumbling wall of opaque glacial water appeared from above, headed straight for Annga, who was farther ahead. She was positioned right in its path, too close to the existing river.

"Annga!" Susi yelled. Annga began to run away, trying to get out of the path of the avalanche of water smashing its way toward her. The water was filled with huge boulders; Susi could see them cracking against each other within the raging waters. Rocks that had been lying dormant since the last ice age hurtled down the mountainside toward Annga.

"Annga, run!" Susi screeched. She was still on the outcropping near where they'd had lunch. She was powerless where she stood. The water made quick work of the distance. Susi could do nothing as she saw the water reach her sister. The wall of water and rocks tumbling within it threw Annga to the ground. Annga's head whipped down, cracking against rock. She was instantaneously enveloped in the silty waters. Her body disappeared completely in the roiling water; not even a glimpse of her brightly coloured jacket told Susi where she had been milliseconds before. Annga's blinking drone-cams zoomed downhill with the rushing waters, presumably following her limp, dead body with their internal sensors.

"Arrgghhh!" Susi screamed. She scrambled away from the torrent as best she could, sobbing. She could barely see through the tears and rainwater soaking her face. She managed to hoist herself onto a large boulder away from the newly formed highway of water just as her legs gave away. A drone zoomed in front of her face. The drone lit up and joyously announced:

YOU'RE THE WINNER!

Saatapiaq
Terrie Kusugak

Saatapiaq only answered questions. Those answers contained five words or less. In the North, as far north as people could survive, his bed was in the doorway of an *iglu*. The caribou skins he slept on he had skinned himself. He never understood how the fur could be so rough and yet soft at the same time. One strand of fur was thick and coarse, yet a whole pelt was soft and warm.

He didn't mind being the outcast. He didn't mind anything as long as he wasn't hungry. When he was small, there was a famine that rolled in like the fog and wiped out everyone but him and three other boys. He knew hunger, the ugly hunger when time reached the sky. He knew he only had to wait five days, five days and the hunger would go away. He imagined that it was because his stomach tightened smaller and smaller until it became a pebble with no room to shrink.

He didn't feel he deserved to miss his parents. Not when he knew their bodies had not been buried. Not when he knew he had to break their femurs to fit them into the pot. Not when he knew he and the other boys felt a great relief at their parents' deaths—a guilty relief. A sickening stripping of meat that left the bones so clean that sunlight reflected in Saatapiaq's eyes. He couldn't tell if it was the light or tears that made him squint. Maybe it was because he only saw them from the corner of his eye, afraid the image of the bones would become the image of their memory. Not the dark, rough skin of the father. A man who could skin three caribou in the time it took his mother to boil the tea. He tried to remember how his father had done it, but the memory was hazy, and he could not be sure if it was a memory or a dream.

He didn't speak to the other three boys, and as far as he knew none of them spoke to each other. The memory was so close to the surface surely one word would unzip these boys head to toe. None of them spoke of the sullen meal, or the shadow that crept over the tundra. So, when the boys started dying, one by one, he made sure to bury their bodies so deep in the ground they could never be found again. The first was Aaliq, nicknamed for his loud, sharp laugh. It was no mystery where he was at any given time, and no mystery why he had to hunt alone, his laugh could be heard over the mountains. His body was found in his iglu. The dome had sunk down like a deflated sealskin buoy. The iglu had melted from the inside, but the *qulliq* was nowhere in sight. Only Saatapiaq and the silent survivors knew the message. When the camp chattered eagerly with gossip, there were many guesses as to how his leg had been snapped in half, severed perfectly. Not at the hip, or the knee, but across the thigh. His leg was gone. The place where his niece sat on his lap, where her tailbone would rest as she was bounced up and down.

Saatapiaq went back to his iglu, silent, always silent; this time there was an eerie look in his eyes, like he was looking into the future, a future where the fog would roll in again. The people that took him in as a child, the ones who found him, were not soft like those who have held a baby in their arms and promised a full life. While Saatapiaq was not loved, he was useful, and that was enough for him. He'd folded kindness long ago. He knew that you could be the most gentle, calm, loving person and be driven to cruelty when your own life hung in the balance. In the same sense, he knew the most cruel person could show great kindness. While he was not hugged and shaped, he was full, he was warm. He preferred the hand-me-down jacket and snowpants. They were well worn, soft in the right places, he didn't mind that the legs were a bit too long and he could feel the tightness in his arms when he lifted them over his head. Eventually the arms would loosen, and the pants folded against his *kamiik*. He knew he'd get taller, like his father, and the pants would be too short in time. The oldest thing he wore was a necklace that belonged to his mother. It was not a man's necklace, but he was not ashamed to wear it. His fingers felt cold when he remembered how his fingertips brushed across his mother's soft skin, gently brushing her hair to the side to take it off her limp body.

The woman of the iglu didn't look up when he walked in. She knew the shuffle of his feet. Saatapiaq immediately saw the water pail was nearly empty. He lifted it onto his shoulder and walked to the lake. He enjoyed his usual trip to the lake. It wasn't very far, but far enough that he could speak to the cranes without being heard. They never replied to him. Cranes came in pairs and looked at him as though they could nearly understand what he was talking about, as if they barley spoke Inuktitut and had to slowly translate the words. He had no word limit with the birds; he never had to worry they would tell a soul, if indeed they had a soul. The Elders said they did, but he had his doubts.

He was surprised when Immak cleared his throat, his polite way of indicating, *I heard what you were saying but I have no intention of mentioning it*. Saatapiaq looked at him with his eyebrows lifted, his way of saying *thank you*. Immak knew he had to start the conversation but didn't know where to start. He looked into Saatapiaq's eyes and realized he could start in the middle. Saatapiaq knew the beginning.

"I think we should tell the Elders," Immak said, his voice deep; it sounded like a whisper.

"We can't," Saatapiaq said. His voice always seemed to crack. He thought perhaps he talked so little his vocal cords rusted.

"I have kids now, Saatapiaq, who knows how far this goes." He looked at the lake as if something was lurking just beneath the surface.

"And Pualuk?" Saatapiaq wondered why Pualuk wasn't here too.

"He's across the bay hunting. He won't be back 'til tomorrow." Immak's voice grew more urgent with each letter.

"Then we wait," Saatapiaq said simply.

"We don't know how long this curse will wait—how did it melt the iglu? Where is the qulliq? We don't know if it's an *ijiraq*, we don't know if it's the spirits, we don't know if our *igluit* are next. My daughter and son sleep in our bed. My wife can't feed them without me. You don't know what it's like to have a real family, to be what keeps your family on this plane." Immak would feel guilty later for rubbing salt in the wound. Saatapiaq's guardians refused to arrange a marriage for him. Well, not so much as refused as said, *We're still looking*.

"We will be banished, anyway," Saatapiaq replied.

Cannibalism was the ultimate crime, for famine came without warning, and panic could turn to frenzy at a moment's notice. Not everyone has the will to wait the five days.

"We were children, surely they will understand. The Elders know of mercy." Immak knew this wasn't a lie. An Elder's knowledge was so deep that to assume their answer was a fool's errand.

"If Pualuk agrees, then I agree," Saatapiaq finally said.

Pualuk would never agree, for in this very moment he was cooling in the snow, his severed leg just an inch from his body.

When Pualuk didn't arrive by the next sunset, Immak told Saatapiaq that he was going to the Elders, and he could join him or not. Saatapiaq followed wordlessly. It was understood Immak would do the talking. It wasn't until Saatapiaq stood before the three oldest Elders that he wondered why the shaman didn't already know the cause of Aaliq's death. Surely he could sense the supernatural presence, and when Immak began speaking, Saatapiaq was certain the shaman knew. When Immak finished speaking the Elders did what they always did when they were disappointed: allowed the silence to grow until the suspense was thick in the air. Let the perpetrators feel the dread and defeat, hearing the failure in their own thoughts before they heard them aloud.

"Find Pualuk, if he still has his *pana* on him you may return." The shaman spoke as if he had deliberated with the other Elders to find a conclusion. Perhaps they had, eye contact was enough when you knew a man a lifetime. Eye contact with Elders was not for the young, it was earned through a lifetime of work, by a man or woman who had tasted death time and again. Those who earned their wrinkled skin. In fact, Saatapiaq's biggest fear was that he could never look an Elder in the eye. That he would become old but never be an Elder, like those lazy men who allowed envy to twist their hearts until their ears shut.

"Why his snow knife?" Immak asked.

"You will understand. Hopefully before it's too late." Neither Saatapiaq nor Immak was surprised by this answer. It was something Elders said when your fate was sealed. When the only direction is forward. The Elder couldn't say, for to tell them was to kill them. The lesson only works if it represents your true character, not some elaborate plan for a loophole. By not telling them, they would forge their own path, not a path marked by the shaman. Only the true path could prove them worthy enough to end the curse, if indeed that's what it was.

They were across the bay before midday, over the valley by mid-afternoon. When they found Pualuk's body, it was already frozen solid. Immak made it there first. Saatapiaq was terrified by Immak's eyes. They showed no grief, only urgency. Immak's knees were barely on the ground before he had his hands all over Pualuk, searching for a knife that he knew in his gut wasn't there. Saatapiaq searched his dogsled. Where the dogs were was a mystery; their tracks had disappeared. Immak and Saatapiaq locked eyes. Immak thought of his children. Saatapiaq thought of the empty water pail left at the lake.

They built an iglu and ate *mikku*, dried caribou that was tough and brittle. The pot filled with evening tea. They slept in shifts, though it turned out that wasn't necessary. Immak shuddered awake when he felt the air get thick and warm. Too warm. Immak ran out of the iglu, angry. He could feel death coming. There was a figure in the distance, its gait not exactly human, but it walked on two feet and stood erect enough that you could tell it had a deep inner thought. It stopped fifty yards out. They couldn't see its face, the dim light and blowing snow had made its figure a blur.

This is a test, Saatapiaq thought. He was not scared. He was not shaking. And that surprised him. Immak was pure instinct. He ran toward the creature, harpoon drawn, each step sure and strong. Saatapiaq stood stuck to the ground. He knew he should follow him and fight, their odds would be better if they fought together, but his feet stayed planted on the ground. Saatapiaq couldn't see Immak's face, didn't see the terror in Immak's eyes, the recognition on the creature's face. Its red eyes confessed its identity. It was an ijiraq—a shapershifter that hid people. The only thing ever left unchanged on an ijiraq was its red eyes, so it always hid its face. Immak jumped so high he could have jumped over Saatapiaq. The harpoon pierced through the ijiraq and it staggered back, not out of pain, but momentum. The ijiraq placed its hands on the blunt end of the harpoon, pushing the weapon through its body and out the other side. Immak fell backward. The ijiraq didn't even kill him before it severed Immak's leg. Blood poured from the limb, freezing as it hit the air, and was solid by the time it hit the ground.

Saatapiaq was sad he wouldn't get to say goodbye to the cranes. Would they miss him? Would they wonder where he went? Or perhaps they wouldn't notice. He didn't run, he didn't want to die face down.

The ijiraq picked up the harpoon and it looked like it was going to throw it and catch Saatapiaq in the chest. Surely it had the strength. Last second, it hammered the harpoon down on the severed leg, picking it up and slinging the whole thing over its shoulder. As the monster walked closer, Saatapiaq realized why its shape was off—slung over his back was Aaliq's leg. When the creature walked over to Pualuk's frozen body, Saatapiaq flinched as the harpoon came down a second time; Immak and Pualuk's legs bounced off one another as the ijiraq lumbered to Saatapiaq.

Saatapiaq accepted his death, for he knew in his heart it was deserved. When the ijiraq stood before him, he realized how tall it was. He recognized the red eyes, or knew what they meant, but nothing could prepare him for the ijiraq's mouth. Its mouth was not horizontal, but vertical, a sideways smile with rotten teeth. The lips full and bright red, a little dimmer than its eyes. It was jarring to see, and Saatapiaq wondered how it would look when it spoke. He wouldn't wait long. Saatapiaq took a deep breath and spoke, his voice clear.

"Would you like to come in for tea?" Saatapiaq offered, as if he were talking to a friend.

The ijiraq was not surprised; it was gleeful. Humans often let their fear get in the way of the fun. This one would be special, it would be his memory, placed in his pocket. He knew he had planned well. Its sickening smile met its nose and the bottom of its chin—Saatapiaq didn't know how he could tell a smile from a frown, but the corners of its lips pointed to its right cheek.

"It would be my pleasure." The ijiraq's face expanded sideways with each vowel. Saatapiaq was torn between looking at its eyes or its teeth. He idly wondered if *ijirait* had baby teeth.

He felt a thickness in the air and crawled into the iglu. The ijiraq followed, even though it seemed too big for the entrance. In fact, it was, but somehow as it passed through the doorway its body would shrink at the edges, a perfect seal of the doorway.

Saatapiaq had started to light his qulliq when the ijiraq put up a hand to stop him. The ijiraq pulled out a qulliq seemingly out of nowhere. It set it down and put Arctic cotton in the shallow bowl of the qulliq. The qulliq was soapstone, shaped like a half moon, the flat side slightly thicker than the curved. The ijiraq put whale oil in the qulliq and let his flint collide; the fire was thick, it was bright as day. Saatapiaq recognized the qulliq. It was a family heirloom, it was Aaliq's qulliq. Saatapiaq was sad it wouldn't be passed down to anyone else. The chain of fire had been broken. Aaliq's son would never warm his iglu with stone carved by his great-great-great grandfather.

The ijiraq lifted Saatapiaq's pot and placed it over the fire. It wordlessly put the limbs on the floor, brought the pana down like an axe, and carefully put the cut legs in the pot. Saatapiaq was ashamed to recognize the smell, and the crack of the bones hurt his ears. Saatapiaq took the tea that was resting on his own qulliq and poured it into two fish-skin cups. He didn't know how he knew the ijiraq liked it cold.

Saatapiaq was not thinking about the murder that had just happened before his eyes. In fact, the memory was thin as a veil. The ijiraq opened its mouth wide and placed the cup close to its chin, poured it backward, and drank. A dibble of tea lingered at the bottom of its lips, and it didn't seem to bother the ijiraq. Saatapiaq knew if he tried to overpower the creature he wouldn't have to worry about the hem of his snowpants. He sensed the ijiraq wanted him to speak, but he knew from the small of his back that it was a trap.

Saatapiaq couldn't take his eyes away from the crooked face. He feared it would change into the face of a demon in his peripherals. The tension bubbled from the boiling pot. The ijiraq looked so excited it was shaking.

It tilted its head to the side, its eyes seeming to have found something. "I thought you would be taller by now." Its voice was a twinning melody, two voices overlapped, the high and the low.

"Have we met?" Saatapiaq felt his body relaxing, the smell no longer bothered him.

"Not officially. But I've seen you grow up. In fact, I saw you born from your mother. I saw your mother when she was born from your grandmother. I am as old as this land." Was its head getting closer or bigger?

"So you saw us starving? You saw them die?" Saatapiaq knew he was supposed to be angry, but his breathing remained steady.

"See, it's such a big deal to you, people are born, and they all die. Do you think your hunger is special? You humans are only on this planet for a wink, you don't know what came before you, what will come after. Just weasels scurrying in the dirt." The ijiraq's eyes darted back and forth, as if it could see the weasels on the floor, following them with its eyes.

"If we are not special, why are you here?" Saatapiaq had spoken more words in this conversation than he had in weeks.

The ijiraq's smile looked like it would split its face in half. "In the beginning—" The qulliq erupted; the fire looked as if it were boiling, moving in unnatural rhythms. Saatapiaq realized it was the opposite of shadow puppets. The flames became people, the ijiraq, the season. "I could sing a song, and draw the children from their beds. Pull a berry picker too far from camp. One child's woe could feed me for years. I was feared, I was respected. Parents warned their children about me. Each human life tasted so sweet, they made me stronger." The ijiraq's nose poked out like a wolf's snout, and like a blink it was gone.

"But I got so strong that one life was not enough. I used to love a team of hunters. Kill three or four, leave one to go home to tell the story. Being a trickster is a full-time job." It continued, its voice, no, *voices,* sunk deeper. "Then I had an idea, an idea no ijiraq had had before. Any monster can take one man, or even three or four, but no ijiraq has ever taken a whole town." The ijiraq searched Saatapiaq's eyes for terror or rage. Instead Saatapiaq looked almost impressed. Saatapiaq was playing a long game, hopefully longer than the ijiraq's.

"But they all died of hunger," the young man said simply.

"Well, who sent the animals away?" It folded its arms triumphantly and sharply nodded its head once. "I don't know if you remember, but the whole town was in a panic, and it got slower and slower as people got hungrier and hungrier. A sluggish peril, a sad parade. I thought the evil would come from the adults, but I should have known it would come from the children. I saw you with your stomach ballooning out, and witnessed the idea sweep across your face. You whispered your plan to the other boys, and one by one they agreed. Immak and Pualuk killed your dad. It took two of them to knock him over, one of them to bring down the harpoon. And you, watching as Aaliq pinned down her arms. You paused wondering if you should slit her throat or stab her in the heart. Aren't you glad you slit her throat? Her heart tasted the best." Its eyes widened, teeth shifting back and forth across its gums like ships on the sea.

Saatapiaq felt a sinking feeling; his strength was wavering. He was starting to feel his resolve wilting through the snow and into the sand. This was the endgame. Death was looming, he was certain. Saatapiaq knew in this moment he would kill anyone to live. A child, a friend, a parent. Anyone, just to live. It should have scared him, he should have felt ashamed, but it gave him resolve. *If I can kill my mother, I can kill an ijiraq.*

"And how did my friends taste?" Saatapiaq asked, the wheels in his mind turning, stalling. He knew he could never overpower the ijiraq, he couldn't outrun it.

The ijiraq smiled. "You'll find out soon, supper is almost ready."

Saatapiaq knew the meat couldn't have boiled to a finish in that time, but somehow it was, for a lack of better words, cooked to perfection. He also knew that if he didn't eat with the ijiraq it would be a slow death. He could feel the ijiraq's thoughts breathing in his mind. The creature was gleeful. Years had led up to this moment. *I'm going to have to eat my friend,* Saatapiaq thought, *on a full stomach this time.*

Saatapiaq steeled his nerves and served himself and the demon. He offered salt out of habit. The ijiraq took it and thanked him.

"Well, eat up, Saatapiaq. Don't want it to get cold. You know what they say, if you kill it you have to eat it."

Saatapiaq smiled wryly, and lifted his closest friend's leg to his mouth and took a bite. It tasted like being a child. It tasted like relief. It tasted like his mother. It was delicious and sickening. *Now, say it now. He's going to kill you.*

"So, would you say you have tasted every animal that has ever existed?" Saatapiaq said, trying hard to sound nonchalant.

The ijiraq could smell something afoot. Another level of the game. "I have tasted every kind of flesh in this world," he said proudly. No one had asked him that before.

"Even..." Saatapiaq tapered off intentionally.

"Yes?" The ijiraq's eyes flashed such a deep red they looked almost black.

"Even ijiraq flesh?" he asked softly.

The ijiraq's face began shaking, his eyes trading places, his mouth turning clockwise until it was back to its normally abnormal crooked smile. "I can't say that I have." The ijiraq's double voice tripled, it became a choir.

"Then you can't say you have tried every flesh in the world. Oh well, close enough." Saatapiaq shrugged, his fear was leaving him. It would be over soon, either way.

"Nor can you, young man. But there is not one around for miles, and it's forbidden among us to kill another equal," it said.

"There is one in here," the human said pointedly.

The ijiraq went still. Everything went still. It was as if the world stopped spinning. They were in a vacuum. *Shit, I'm dead,* Saatapiaq thought to himself. But the ijiraq breathed out a laugh, and time moved again with it.

"I'll trade you; a leg for a leg," it said. The ijiraq knew Saatapiaq would never agree. He was not sure which he wanted, to keep his leg, or to fully corrupt this boy. He could change his leg, he could be a bear, or bird, or fox, but once it was gone, there was no growing it back. He couldn't shake the thought, the feeling, the need to know—*What does an ijiraq taste like?*

"That sounds fair," Saatapiaq agreed.

The ijiraq was almost floating with shock and joy. *The boy was stupid enough to play?*

They spoke at the same time, the same words. "Who first?" Saatapiaq's voice was added to the myriad voices of the ijiraq. The crooked creature liked the idea of this boy's voice being added to his own. The ijiraq put one arm behind his back and said, "If you can guess what shape my hand has taken you can decide who goes first."

Saatapiaq felt dread run through him, weighing him down. *This creature will lie. This creature can change his hand in a second. By the time he reveals his hand he can change it a hundred times over,* Saatapiaq thought.

The ijiraq could feel his hesitation and reached a compromise. "Well then, how about this. You close your eyes, and I'll put my palm—well, someone's palm—in your hand and if you can guess whose it is, you win. I'll even say, it's the hand of someone you have met." The ijiraq raised his hand to demonstrate his skill. It was small, a child's arm, then it was large and dark brown with thick fingers. Again and again different hands flashed before him, connected to the shoulder of a sick creature.

Saatapiaq nodded and closed his eyes. It felt wrong to take his eyes off the monster but he fought his instinct and kept them shut. He held his hands open and offered them to the ijiraq. He felt smooth skin softly touch his own and cursed himself. *How often do you remember someone's hands?* This would be impossible. *Show no fear, remember this is a game. He wouldn't choose someone random— that would be no fun. This is someone I know; this is someone I love.* The ijiraq gave a gentle squeeze and it felt so familiar Saatapiaq began to cry.

"This is my mother's hand." He was grateful and disgusted. Blessed to have his mother's touch; horrified that it was not his mother.

The ijiraq chortled a deep chuckle. "That was an easy one."

He meant for me to guess right, there is a reason. Saatapiaq could feel his mother's hand growing cold, just as it had when she died. He looked up and saw his mother's face on top of a monster, the only difference was the creepy red eyes, the colour of blood. Her blood. Once he let go of her hand his mother's face disappeared.

"I win, you first." Saatapiaq handed the ijiraq his pana. The monster took it and for a moment Saatapiaq was sure he was going to be stabbed. The ijiraq raised the knife and brought it down hard on his own femur with a sickening crack. The blood that gushed from his limb was a rotten red-black. The fire in the qulliq blazed so hot the iglu began to melt, pictures of light surrounded them. The images showed the day that they killed their own people. The ijiraq took the qulliq and pressed the hot end to his wound and cauterized it. The pictures disappeared with the fire. He lit the qulliq again, put his own leg in the pot, and handed Saatapiaq the knife. Saatapiaq lifted the knife high above his head and brought it down into the ijiraq's heart.

"*Utsuuk!*" he cursed with a thousand voices. "That's not fair!" The ijiraq gurgled, and just one voice emerged. Its true voice. It was gravely and older than time. It considered killing the boy now. It would be simple. The boy didn't run away, he couldn't. The ijiraq's power held him there, but there were worse punishments than death. The ijiraq felt death in itself and it was exciting, a new chapter, its first death. That was the only new thing left for it. Well, almost. It still hadn't tasted ijiraq flesh. "Give me a final request. Feed me. Feed myself to me, to us. Share with me my last meal."

Saatapiaq, for a reason not even known to himself, began to serve them both. He was in a trance, he felt his most sickening self coming to the surface. In some twisted way he was curious to taste what no one else has ever tasted. The ijiraq smiled; maybe they would both get their way.

The pair lifted the meat to their lips and took a bite. It tasted like time. It tasted like fear and ecstasy. It tasted of every memory, every itch and scratch of the ijiraq's life. They both had visions of birth and murder, cruelty and peace. It lasted a lifetime, it lasted a second. In a blink they were back in the melted iglu. The ijiraq's red eyes dulled, they went black, then grey, then empty. The creature's body slumped to the ground, no longer a body but a mass, a black gooey mass. It seeped into the snow, into the ground, into the earth, back where it came from.

Saatapiaq breathed a sigh of relief. He was alive and the monster was dead and now he was totally alone. He took the large knife and started walking home. The Elder would need to see it. As he walked, his stomach tightened and spun and he felt dizzy. His mouth was tingling and dry. Apparently ijiraq meat didn't sit well in human bodies. He knelt on the sea ice to drink from a melted shallow pool—really more of a puddle. It was cold and glassy and he saw in his own reflection eerie red eyes. The shock stopped his breath. Then he felt the pain. His face was breaking and healing and re-breaking. His teeth were migrating. His jaw was shifting. His eyes were the only thing to stay in place, until his mouth was sideways.

There was fear, pain, longing in his eyes. He knew what he had to do, but his resolve was weak. He couldn't do it alone, he needed someone. He needed his mother. He closed his eyes and remembered her face, her body, her smell, and willed it outside of himself. *Please, please, please,* he chanted over and over in his mind. He opened his eyes and saw not his face but his mother's reflection. He looked at her with such love, and when it was mirrored back to himself he almost forgot that it was not his mother staring back at him. Almost. But he ignored the red eyes and pretended. He took the snow knife to his own throat, never losing sight of his mother, even as his blood dyed the water red. He smiled, for he could see his mother one last time.

The Power Outage

Micah Silu Inutiq

Qiluya woke to a firm nudge. Her *anaana*'s voice, low and urgent, broke through her haze of sleep. "We're here," she said, her brown eyes filled with worry.

Rubbing her eyes, Qiluya crawled out of the cramped cabin of their boat, greeted by the biting cold and the scent of salt in the air. The wind stung her face, waking her up as she surveyed their surroundings. The familiar landscape of Tasiujakuluk came into view. The rolling hills, splashed with the reds and oranges of a new season, felt wrong somehow. She should be at school right now, huddled outside with her other teenage friends at recess. Instead, the familiar beach of her childhood lay ahead, its pale sand stretching toward their blue cabin, which sat just above the high tide mark, propped up by stacks of driftwood. Beyond it, the tundra lay untouched, crowberries ripe and ready for picking. A telltale sign of fall. As the boat lurched onto the shallows of the shore, cries of snow buntings and seagulls rose in alarm, acknowledging their arrival.

Qiluya and her family worked in silence, moving bags from the boat to the cabin with a quiet urgency. They had brought more supplies than usual, which had been packed in a hurry in the middle of the night.

As Qiluya and her mother began to unpack the many boxes they had brought, she stopped to look out the window toward the shore, where her older brother, Isaiah, helped their *ataata* untangle the seal net. His movements, she noticed, were slow and distracted. She could see the tension in his shoulders and the way his gaze kept drifting south, toward the friends and family they had left behind.

Panic had swept through their community the night before, only a week after a mysterious power outage shut everything down across their town. At first, the community seemed hardly affected, power outages were common in the North, but not usually for this long. The first few days, families shared food and supplies as everyone relished their unexpected break from work and school. But on the fourth day, when the internet went down, whispers spread from one household to the next that the powerplant workers were missing. Ricky, the town's sole resident cop tried to investigate. But his own fear quickly overwhelmed him, despite his supposed extensive training, when he found the power corp's office abandoned. No one had seen the workers in days.

On the fifth day, the one flight from the city didn't show up. Anxiety amongst the community grew as the produce at the only grocery store withered away.

On the sixth day, Ataata's older cousin Sully arrived on an ATV, his broad frame and weathered face made him look even more rugged than usual. A seasoned hunter from a neighbouring town, Sully had the kind of presence that made people listen, even when he didn't say much. A cigarette, always half smoked, hung out of the side of his mouth.

"Hi, Anaana," he said in his deep, gentle voice, pinching Qiluya's cheek as she greeted him outside her house. She was named after his late mother, whom she'd never had the chance to meet.

"You guys got power out, too?" he asked as he lit another cigarette, his large hands blocking the wind from the flame. Ataata emerged from his shed, his thick eyebrows furrowed in surprise to see his normally reclusive cousin.

"Hey, we got a problem, Cuz," Uncle Sully warned, his voice dropping. Ataata didn't ask any questions. He knew by the look in Uncle Sully's eyes that whatever he was going to say wasn't good.

"In the shed," Ataata said quietly. "Qiluya, you go inside."

Qiluya nodded as she watched the two men enter the shed and close the door behind them. When it was closed, she quietly snuck around the back to a small crack in the wood she used to eavesdrop. She pressed her ear to the crack.

"It's not good, Cuz," Uncle Sully warned. "I found those two powerplant guys way out past the big island."

"Were they ok? What the hell were they doing out there?" Ataata asked in surprise.

"They weren't doing anything when I found them . . ." Uncle Sully's voice saddened, trailed off into silence.

"Shit," Ataata grumbled as he let out a loud sigh and paced around the shed.

"I'm telling you, something's not right, Cuz. I've been seeing things lately, more than usual . . . things that *Ataatatsiaq* used to warn us about. At first it was only far inland, but I've been noticing them hunt closer and closer to the towns," Uncle Sully warned.

"Noticing *what* hunt, Sully boy?" Ataata asked, almost upset, not believing his cousin.

"Just trust me. The earlier you guys get out of here, the better."

Ataata fell silent for a long moment before Uncle Sully quietly said, "Here, take these. Ataatatsiaq taught me how to make them—"

"These are just trinkets he made to pass the time, Sully boy. They don't actually mean anything," Ataata interrupted, impatience growing in his voice.

"Look," Uncle Sully responded, "Ataatatsiaq told me that one day I would need to pass on what he taught me, to help our family. That it was a burden he knew I would be able to handle. You don't have to believe me, Cuz. But if Ataatatsiaq had given these to you to protect the family, would you have questioned him?"

After a long pause, Ataata finally whispered, " . . . No." A hint of sadness trailed in his voice.

Qiluya got up quietly and crept away, feeling uneasy. She didn't fully understand everything she had heard, but Uncle Sully was the most knowledgeable of the land out of anyone she knew, and she trusted his word. *What did he mean by 'they were hunting closer to town'?* Qiluya wondered. *Was it bears? But what would they have to do with the power outage?* It didn't make sense. That evening, Uncle Sully stayed for dinner, but left quickly, eager to return to the land where he seemed most at ease—away from people.

On the seventh day, news spread that the powerplant guys had died on the land, where Uncle Sully had found them. Whatever remaining calm there was in town dissolved as families stricken with grief began to fight over space and food, realizing they were alone in a town with no power, no food, no law, and no way of communicating with the outside world. By midnight, the grocery store had been ransacked amongst the desperation and fear that had spread. There was no one to stop it.

Qiluya's ataata hadn't waited for things to get worse. As soon as the first shouts echoed through the streets, he woke up Isaiah and loaded the boat with all the gas and supplies they could find. By sunrise, they were already on the water, driving away from town. "Don't look back," Ataata scolded when Qiluya and her little sister Cookie turned to see a dark column of smoke rising from the health centre. Qiluya swallowed a lump in her throat and looked away. It was all too much. As they left the boundaries of town, she looked back at Mr. Jonah's house, which was the last house on the northern edge of town before the land stretched out for hundreds of miles. It had been boarded up and abandoned since he passed away last month. They were moving quickly on the water, but Qiluya thought she could make out a face in the window of Mr. Jonah's old house. It appeared to be someone wearing the mask of a caribou, its large antlers outstretched above its face. Qiluya looked away, unease growing in her chest. She saw a handful of other families who were leaving as well and came to the sad realization that it was the ones left behind, the ones who couldn't escape to the safety of the land, who would be consumed by the chaos.

A scream broke through Qiluya's thoughts.

"Where's my Ninu!?" Cookie's frantic cries cut through the cabin, her tiny hands rummaging through the boxes scattered everywhere. Her stuffed bear wasn't there. "I want my Ninu!" Cookie sobbed, her small body shaking as Anaana scooped her into her arms, trying to calm her.

"I'll go check the boat, *Nuka*," Qiluya reassured, slipping on her parka as her mother nodded in thanks. Stepping outside, she felt cold raindrops land on her freckled skin. Fog was rolling in from the ocean, thick and heavy.

Qiluya followed the trail her family had walked from the boat as her boots felt the satisfying crunch of rotting seaweed beneath, her face suddenly scrunched in disgust as a foul odour invaded her senses. It was sulfuric, like a neglected sealskin left in the sun. Her eyes darted around, both looking for Ninu and the source of the smell. Qiluya stopped as she spotted some tracks in the sand. They were caribou tracks . . . but the size of the hooves didn't make sense; they were as big as polar bear paw prints. As she followed the trail with her eyes, she saw that it led to her cabin. She noted that there seemed to be only two prints instead of four. She shook her head and turned back to the water. In the distance, she could see Isaiah and Ataata in their *qajaak*, setting the seal net in deeper water. After climbing aboard the boat in the shallow water, Qiluya rummaged through the boat's compartments, her heart racing for reasons she couldn't explain. Finally, she spotted Ninu laying on a blanket in the cabin. "Got you!" she muttered in relief, clutching the bear tightly.

As she climbed out, Qiluya heard a familiar voice call her name.

"I found it, Anaana!" Qiluya shouted back. But she heard it again, clearer this time, "*Qiluya!*"

Qiluya froze and her eyes widened. "Hannah? Is that you!?" she called out, searching for the source of her friend's voice.

"Over here!" Hannah's voice echoed from beyond the cabin. In the distance, Qiluya thought she could make out the small frame of her best friend, Hannah.

Without thinking, Qiluya sprinted, her heart pounding harder with each step as she passed her cabin.

"Hurry!" Hannah's voice urged her on, pulling her further away from the safety of her family.

Qiluya kept running, over the hill behind her cabin and toward the large lake that lay just beyond it. She stopped at the water's edge, hands on her knees, trying to catch her breath.

"Hannah?" she muttered, looking around. A single loon paddled in the lake and let out a trembling call. It vaguely sounded like Hannah. A gust of wind almost blew Qiluya over, and she swore she could hear a giggle as it moved over her and toward her cabin. A chill ran down Qiluya's spine. She had the sense of being watched. She looked around, trying to identify what it could be and turned back to the lake where the loon had been swimming. It was gone.

This isn't right, am I going crazy? Qiluya thought, shaking her head as her mother's voice cut through the air, commanding and urgent.

"Qiluya! Where are you?"

"Anaana, it's Hannah!" she yelled back, confused.

"COME BACK HERE. NOW," her mother boomed, leaving no room for argument.

Reluctantly, Qiluya turned and started walking back, her feet dragging. Surely, her Anaana would want to help Hannah, too? As she neared the cabin, another faint, chilling laugh drifted through the wind. The fog had swallowed the landscape now, and the sight of her family's warm cabin, glowing softly from within, was the only thing grounding her. Her stomach growled and she was very thirsty.

She stepped inside. The smell of hot bannock filled the small space. Her family was gathered on the floor, carpeted with cardboard, a feast of seal meat, bannock, and fresh berries spread out. Her stomach growled, but her mind was still spinning.

"Where did you go?" her anaana scolded, her voice sharp with fear.

"Look! I found Ninu!" Qiluya said quickly, handing the bear to Cookie, who squealed in delight.

"You've been gone for hours," her mother continued, her eyes filled with a mixture of anger and worry.

"What? No, I wasn't," Qiluya replied, confused. "I heard Hannah, so I went to find—"

Her parents shared a worried look before her Ataata's deep voice interrupted, "That wasn't Hannah, *Panik*."

Qiluya's heart skipped a beat. "Ataata? But I heard her, I swear—"

"Look at me," he said, his voice hard, his gaze locking onto hers. His eyes brimmed with worry. He continued, "That was something else. Isaiah, Qiluya, listen to me closely. There's something happening out there right now, and we can't trust everything we see and hear, okay? We need to use our common sense. I know things are uncertain, but we have to stick together. Everything will be okay."

The words sent a jolt of fear through Qiluya. Tears welled in her eyes as the weight of the past day crashed down on her. She ran to the bunk bed, burying her face in her arms as she let the fear and uncertainty out in quiet sobs.

Hours later, Qiluya awoke. The soft glow of solar lights barely cut through the thick darkness inside the cabin. Her parents were sitting at the kitchen table, their voices hushed but tense. Isaiah snored softly on the couch, Cookie curled up beside him. The fog outside pressed against the windows.

"We can't stay here forever," Anaana whispered, her voice strained. "We'll run out of food in a few weeks."

"If things are still too bad in town, we'll survive like Inuit always have, until things get better. I just need to fix the VHF and we can get ahold of the other families," Ataata replied, his voice sounding more tired than reassuring.

"It's not the same now," Anaana argued, shaking her head. "We don't have as much knowledge as the Inuit who came before us."

Qiluya sat up, catching their attention. "Hi," she whispered.

"Hi, Panik. Come here," her mother said, opening her arms. Qiluya crawled onto her anaana's lap, letting herself be held like a child again. Her ataata sighed, rubbing his beard in frustration.

"I'll heat up your food, Panik. You need to eat," he muttered, pushing himself up from the table. But before he could take another step, there was a knock at the door.

All three of them froze in place. "Ataata?" Qiluya whimpered, her voice trembling as her anaana held her tightly.

"Silah, take the girls upstairs. NOW," her ataata commanded quietly. Anaana rushed to scoop Cookie into her arms before climbing up the foldable ladder to the loft. Qiluya followed behind quickly, her heart racing as her ataata grabbed his gun. The loft stairs creaked as he folded them back up, closing his wife and daughters in safely above.

Ataata woke up Isaiah, who was groggy but quickly alert. "Someone knocked on the door. If I go outside, do NOT follow me, no matter what you hear. There are tricksters out there," Ataata instructed, handing Isaiah a rifle and a small object that Isaiah stuffed in his pocket.

The Power Outage | 133

"It's probably just someone we know," Isaiah muttered, trying to sound calm, but the fear in his voice betrayed him.

"It's going to be okay," Ataata promised aloud, before walking over and opening the door slowly, gun at the ready. Ataata peaked his head out and found no one. He nodded to Isaiah and stepped outside into the fog.

In the loft, Qiluya lay trembling, her mother softly stroking her hair, trying to soothe her. After what seemed like a long time, Qiluya's tears gave way to exhaustion, and she drifted off into a restless sleep.

When Qiluya awoke, she could hear her father whistling downstairs. The loft stairs had been lowered and she climbed down cautiously. The rancid smell from the day before had returned. Her ataata was at the counter, cheerfully making breakfast. Isaiah was nowhere to be seen.

"Hi, Panik!" Ataata called out, his voice unnervingly upbeat.

"Hi . . ." Qiluya responded, her unease growing. "What's going on?"

"Nothing to worry about," Ataata replied with a too-bright smile. "Everything's fine. It was nothing last night. Breakfast is almost ready," he said as he portioned torn pieces of a raw ptarmigan, feathers included, onto plates.

Qiluya hesitated, a twinge of fear rising from her stomach. She looked around. "W-where's Isaiah?"

Ataata paused, turning slowly to face her, an unnatural smile spreading across his face—one that didn't reach his eyes as he chewed on a piece of the meat. "He's getting the boat ready. We're moving to the old camp today."

"The old camp?" Qiluya frowned. "But that's hours from here . . . and no one's been there in years. Why are we going there?"

"I got the VHF working last night," Ataata said, almost too enthusiastically. "That's where the other families are now. I even spoke to Hannah's Ataata—they're all there, safe and sound!"

Qiluya felt a strange mix of relief and confusion. The thought of seeing her best friend again brightened her mood, but something about her Ataata didn't sit right.

She looked over at Anaana, who was packing Cookie's toys in a bag. She seemed far more reserved than usual, while Ataata's overly cheerful demeanor was unsettling.

As Qiluya lifted a box to bring to the boat, she hesitated. "Ataata . . . who knocked on the door last night?"

"Oh . . . that was just Mr. Jonah checking on us," Ataata said with a dismissive wave as he packed the final box.

Qiluya's stomach dropped. She nodded quietly and turned toward the boat, feeling bile climb up her throat. Mr. Jonah was dead, and Ataata knew that. He was an Elder whom Ataata respected greatly.

Ataata's words from the day before echoed in her head: *That was something else.*

When she reached the boat, she handed the box to Isaiah, his face etched with worry, mirroring her own. "Isaiah . . ." she whispered, her voice tight with fear. "What happened last night?"

Isaiah's eyes darted nervously. He swallowed hard before speaking. "I waited for hours, Qilu," he said, his voice shaking. "And . . . I thought I heard Cin calling for me. I . . . I almost went outside." He trailed off, ashamed, as Anaana approached, Cookie tucked in her *amauti*. Cin was his girlfriend who had still been in town when they left.

"Get on the boat, Qilu," Isaiah urged quietly. Qiluya nodded and did as she was told.

The Power Outage | 135

Anaana's pace quickened, her face pale as she waded into the shallows. As soon as she reached the boat, she began to push it back before jumping on. Isaiah revved the motor. Anaana's hands were trembling as she covered her mouth. Qiluya's heart raced as their ataata emerged from the cabin, roaring with fury as he realized they were trying to leave without him.

"Wait!" Qiluya screamed, panic rising in her chest. "What are you doing!" she screamed at Isaiah.

"Qilu," Isaiah said, his voice low as he met her eyes. "That's not Ataata. Whatever came back into the cabin last night . . . that wasn't him."

Qiluya blinked, fear and confusion flooding her mind. "What are you talking about?" she asked.

Isaiah nodded toward the cabin of the boat. "Look," he whispered.

Qiluya's eyes widened, and her breath caught in her throat as she bent over and peered inside the cabin of the boat. There, huddled in the corner, pale and shivering, was Ataata. His face was as pale as Anaana's. Qiluya took a step back in disbelief. If Ataata was here, then . . . who had just come out of their cabin?

She turned slowly, her heart pounding as her eyes followed her anaana's, which were locked onto the figure on the shore. The shape of her ataata—no, the thing—was morphing, its body stretching unnaturally. Antlers sprouted from its head, twisted and misshapen, while its face contorted into something grotesque and monstrous. It was a caribou, but it stood on two legs, moving in ways that no living creature should.

"Qiluya! Come back and play!" it screamed, its voice shifting, mimicking Hannah's. The sound crackled and crawled up her spine.

The source of the voice was now made horrifyingly clear. She had only heard of them in children's books. Shapeshifters. Tricksters. Beings that lured people away from safety.

"*Ijiraq* . . ." Qiluya whispered in horror, turning to her mother, her voice barely audible.

Her anaana nodded, her face etched with horror as they sped away, the boat cutting through the water, leaving behind the creature that had worn her ataata's face. The real Ataata emerged from the cabin of the boat.

"But how?" Qiluya started, her voice trembling. Isaiah rummaged through his pocket and pulled out the object that Ataata had gifted him the night before and showed it to Qiluya. It was a small ivory figurine wrapped in polar bear fur.

"Uncle Sully gave these to Ataata before he left. Check your pocket," Isaiah said.

Qiluya searched her pockets with trembling hands and found the object that had saved them. She looked at Anaana, who was holding another one. They had been protected all along, without even knowing it.

Ataata pulled out his figurine. "Last night, I almost got lost in the fog. I wandered in circles for a long time and heard all sorts of strange voices. Some familiar, childhood friends, animals, the sound of different weather. The ijiraq . . . it tried to lure me away, but this little thing, it kept the ijiraq away," he said as he inspected the object. "I waited in the boat all night, trying to figure out what to do until Isaiah showed up. I don't think the ijiraq was used to being the one getting tricked. Sully boy was right . . ." he said, guilt in his voice as he looked to the now distant shore of Tasiujakuluk. "My ataatatsiaq used to make these for us as kids. As protection against evil and injuries. I always thought it was just a silly thing he did to make himself feel we were safe..."

Qiluya blinked away tears as she hugged her ataata tightly, realizing how close they had come to losing him. "We're safe now, Panik," Ataata said gently as he hugged her in return. "Uncle Sully said he'd wait for us at the big island camp in case things ... weren't safe."

As the boat sped away in the morning mist, Qiluya's eyes drifted back to the shore in the distance, where the ijiraq's call echoed faintly across the water, a stark lesson that the *ijirait* had always been there. Waiting to prey upon those who had forgotten. A society that had forgotten.

Utiqtuq: Chapter 2

Gayle Uyagaqi Kabloona

Trigger warning: This story contains suicidal ideation.

ALIISA HAD BEEN IN A HELICOPTER CRASH.

Just before that, she'd made the hardest decision of her young life.

She had been living on the land with Ittuq, a grandfather figure who'd taught her everything she needed to know about survival, and Anirniq, a five-year-old who didn't speak after the traumas he'd endured in the outbreak. They lived basically the same way their ancestors had lived: in tents and *igluit*, following game animals and seasonal changes.

Only now, they had to be on guard against *ijiraujait*.

When Aliisa was turning twelve, a global pandemic had turned most of the population into half-dead, slathering, zombie-like creatures. Inuit called them "ijiraujait" after the traditional legend. According to oral history, hunters would go out on the land and see a healthy game animal moving in the distance. Once shot, the hunter would approach the animal to find a decomposing corpse: blackened skin, meat rotten and sinking into the ground. Ijiraujait would lure hunters far away into a dangerous chase, bridging the distance between the dead and living.

Aliisa had watched the world fall apart, supply chains destroyed, transportation routes terminated, her loved ones turned into bloodthirsty, ravenous monsters—but she had survived.

Aliisa, Ittuq, and Anirniq shared a camp on the western edge of Baffin Island. Earlier that morning a doctor had arrived at their camp in a helicopter. He told them that a vaccine had been developed and treatment plans made available for recently turned ijiraujait. Aliisa had jumped at the opportunity to return to her home with them. She had to know if anyone she knew had survived like her. She missed the modern comforts of living in a permanent settlement, being warm all the time, showers, food options, people her age, entertainment. . . . She was flying into the unknown yet again, with Anirniq by her side.

Ittuq had warned her that the *qallunaat* didn't always know what was best. Ittuq had been taken from his family and their traditional lifestyle when he was a child and had ended up in a residential school. He spent much of his life being told that the Southern lifestyle was far superior to Inuit life and culture. Ittuq didn't trust the doctor when he showed up with the good news. He elected to stay at their camp by himself, refusing to give up his lifestyle yet again, especially after the world he'd been forced to adopt had ended so brutally.

Aliisa should have listened to him.

Aliisa didn't see it coming when the helicopter pilot's virus blocker medication failed in the cold Arctic environment. How could she? She was thirteen years old. She trusted what the doctor told her, she believed that adults had all the answers. She didn't know that the treatment had been put together so quickly that the few scientists left in the world hadn't tested it in diverse environmental conditions. The ingredients separated in the cold Nunavut conditions and became inert, which led to her current terrible situation.

They hadn't been in the air long when the pilot reverted to his infected state. He attacked the doctor in the passenger's seat, abandoning his driving controls.

So Aliisa found herself amid yet another catastrophe. The helicopter had begun an erratic spin, and they crashed violently on the rocky shore and shallow waters of a tidal flat. Aliisa momentarily lost consciousness. As she woke, she heard screams and frantic pounding noises. Her head throbbed and her ears rang from the impact of the crash. She was strewn with bits of glass from the broken window beside her.

Before her brain fully realized what was happening, the pilot had slithered halfway out of his seatbelt, hands like claws grasping at a half-conscious Anirniq in the backseat beside her. The doctor in the front seat was bitten to pieces, covered in blood, and convulsing as the virus worked its way through his nervous system. She scrambled with her safety straps, trying to get away from the tornado of danger whirling before her. She screeched uncontrollably when the pilot finally worked his way out of his belt and lunged at Anirniq. He was still helplessly buckled into his seat. The pilot bit relentlessly at his face and neck. When Anirniq's arms flailed in an effort to protect himself, the pilot simply bit at them too. Aliisa's hands desperately clawed at the buckle, finally setting herself free. Blood squirted in all directions as the pilot bit through Anirniq's carotid artery. Aliisa threw herself headfirst out of the broken window.

She landed rough on the rocks below. The hand intended to break her fall crumpled. Her shoulder took the rest of her weight, and her head hit the side of a rock. She tumbled once more and came to a rest with her limbs splayed across the muck and wet sea rocks. She winced and attempted to sit up. Blood dripped from the gash on her head. She tried to move, but the lower half of her left leg was bent at an alarming angle and not cooperating. Through the shooting pain, she told herself to move quickly if she wanted to survive this.

The head of what was once the pilot appeared framed in the window Aliisa had just escaped from. Its eerily wide eyes bored holes into her. Blood stained its face everywhere but a ring around those laser-focused eyes, its mouth open and panting. Aliisa moved, frightened into action, ignoring the pain in her leg and hand. She quickly grabbed a rock with her good hand. She crouched with her rock-wielding hand cocked. The *ijiraujaq* sailed snapping toward her.

In an instant, the creature was within swinging distance. Aliisa's rock struck out to meet it, colliding with perfect timing on the ijiraujaq's temple. Aliisa took a fast sidestep to allow its body to sail right by her, carried by its frenzied momentum. Thankfully the body was now limp—whatever physiology the virus animated had been switched off by brute force. The body's writhing and jerking stopped.

And lucky for Aliisa, too, because she'd sidestepped onto her injured leg, painfully fallen again, and sat back gasping at the air. When she looked down to assess herself, she let out a guttural scream. Her ankle was bent at an even more shockingly steep angle, bone poking through the skin of her shin. Her socks and pants were torn up the leg. She yowled, clutching the injured leg. She looked up at the sky. The sun felt like a spotlight, and with the adrenalin coursing through her veins, the colours of the surrounding rock and tundra in the distance were amplified. Each strand of seaweed strewn about her seemed to burn a pattern into the back of her eyes.

Her eyes pooled and spilled with fat tears as she sobbed. She heard the terrifying noises of active ijiraujait coming from the helicopter. But now the grunting and howling she heard was from the body of what was once her small, sweet, and quiet Anirniq. He had been the breath of fresh air she and Ittuq needed most when they found him. Now, instead, she scrambled across wet rocks and mud to get away from him. She felt as if her heart had been torn out of her body. For a moment, the flashing, blinding pain paralyzed her.

She was filled with regret for not being able to help Anirniq, and for leaving Ittuq. More than anything, she wished she hadn't left. She felt betrayed by these qallunaat who had offered her promises of a repaired world, and she was livid at herself for bringing the one person whose safety she was responsible for. She was eaten up inside, alone again. It felt like how things had been when she'd first escaped Iqaluit—before she'd found Ittuq—or worse. She looked around and gave in to the hopelessness and dread; she let herself sob into the ground she laid upon.

But she didn't have time to let herself wallow in her situation. Those sounds from the ijiraujaq in the crushed metal vehicle reminded her she needed to make moves. She mustered everything she had left and worked out a half crawl/half drag and hop on her good leg while she oscillated between despair and determination. She made very slow headway from the coast into the interior of the island. She needed to get back to Ittuq—he was the closest person to her and the only salvation she knew.

She knew how to navigate on the open land. The weather was on her side, at least, sunny and dry. The sun was high enough that there was hope. They were only in the beginnings of fall. Aliisa wished desperately for Ittuq's help, or for her rifle back at camp: the one the qallunaat had told her she wouldn't need, that she wasn't allowed to wield, because she was "just a child"....

Ittuq watched the helicopter take off with the only family he had left. There was no way he trusted those qallunaat, not as far as he could throw them. He was angry with them for showing up, filled with false promises of a better life. Ittuq didn't believe that something like the sickness that made ijiraujait could be controlled. He'd seen too many of them, been chased, fought and shot his way to safety in isolation on the *nuna*. He thought what he'd shared with Aliisa and Anirniq hadn't been so bad. They had freedom, they could hunt and catch food, they had each other to rely on. It was calm compared to what they'd all seen as the sickness worked its way north and society failed.

Ittuq hated thinking about the past. When possible, he lived in the present and felt gratitude for the things that he had. He didn't think about the family he'd lost, the first time or the second time. The first, when he'd been taken from his family and nomadic life on the nuna and put in residential school; the second, when he escaped town, running from the ijiraujait. If he started thinking about all the things he'd lost in his life, the strong barriers he'd built over a lifetime would begin to collapse. He never let himself open up to those emotions.

When he'd found Anirniq and Aliisa, he'd poured his heart and soul into those kids. He taught his vast life skills to them to keep them safe. He protected them fiercely and gave them instruction and enough leeway to gain independence and confidence in their own abilities.

Aliisa had turned out to be incredibly capable. She had spent most of her pre-pandemic life in town, but learned quickly and flourished with Ittuq's instruction. Anirniq was young and never spoke, but he was excellent on watch, his eyes constantly scanning the horizon.

Aliisa and Ittuq had named the little one Anirniq, which means "breath" or "spirit" because he brought them life—and because he wouldn't or couldn't tell them his name. They'd found him all alone; somehow, he'd survived the ijiraujait attacks that must have come for his family. Aliisa and Ittuq loved and spoiled him, the youngest and most special of them all. They both half-believed he was sent to lift their spirits and give them reason to go on. They gave him the best pieces of game meat and *kuniit* every day.

What would Ittuq do with himself now? He was alone and heartbroken. Plus, he was more in danger of attack alone. He wouldn't have anyone to share night watch. His vision wasn't as good as it had been. Dusk was hard, shapes materialized out of shadows and morphed into dangers that vanished when he looked closer. He didn't fear being out in nature . . . but then again, ijiraujait weren't natural.

Forlorn and without purpose, he wandered out with his rifle. He walked and walked, the only way he was ever able to make sense of the world, whichever world he was forced into. The sun ran its daily course, from high in the sky to deep in the west.

His instincts from a lifetime of hunting game told him to climb the tallest hill nearby. He stood atop the *qinngummivik* watching the setting sun and felt the light breeze against his face. He wondered why he'd been the one to weather all these changes. He'd survived so much, seen friends and family succumb to the effects of colonialism, old age, sickness, or become ijiraujait. And for what? To end up alone on a hill with nothing to go back to at camp. He wondered briefly if he should have followed Aliisa and Anirniq, but caught himself. He loved those kids, but there was nothing left for him in the life they were headed to. If there was one thing he knew, it was that he belonged here on the land.

Aliisa had fought past feeling sorry for herself. She was dragging her bloody and broken body across the tundra. She tried to use her broken leg, quickly gave up, and instead crawled, using her forearms and good leg. Her injured leg dragged behind, bouncing painfully against the ground.

She had turned her pain into determination. She was not going out like this, not after everything she'd been through. She had the wild look of a dying animal—which she was. She had made small progress, but it was progress, nonetheless. She grunted along, heaving hard, sweating with exertion even as the temperature turned cold. She was forced to stop frequently and catch her breath. If she banged her injured leg particularly hard, she hollered into the ground, punching and yelling like it was the earth's fault.

The sun was setting on Ittuq as he contemplated going on. He didn't realize its depth, but he had slipped into a deep, existential depression. He couldn't see a reason for continuing. He had stayed on the top of the qinngummivik replaying moments of his life. He had no reason to return to camp. He was hungry but didn't care. Terrible memories forced themselves to the forefront of his brain, plastering themselves over any happy moments he'd ever had. He felt like a black hole was making its way through the timeline of his life, attracting series of traumas to him. The more he struggled onward in life, the more hardships he ran into.

He was distracted from his dark thoughts by a series of strange noises. He sighed, knowing that strange noises meant an ijiraujaq was nearby. The threat of imminent death sparked a small reflexive feeling of self-preservation. He walked slowly down the hill toward the sound, stopping every once in a while to hone in on the sounds.

Dusk had begun, the worst time for Ittuq's bad eyesight. Of course an ijiraujaq encounter would happen during this time—more bad luck on top of a worse day. He spotted a dark, slow-moving silhouette that must have been making all the noise in the distance. He could just make out enough of it to see it was pulling itself along the ground on its stomach. Easy to take care of. They're much easier to get rid of when they're not running at you. He'd only need to walk up and extinguish it.

"Forced out of my thoughts only to kill," he muttered to himself and sighed. "Not exactly a boost in morale." He thought about what would happen if he didn't kill this one. No one would ever know what happened to him at the end. And now it didn't matter to anyone if he was gone.

He walked toward the creature, no longer afraid of it attacking him. He'd found many ijiraujait like this one, so damaged that they could barely propel themselves toward their human prey. He came to a safe distance a few metres from the body. It had stopped clawing its way forward. It was a pale and ragged mess: torn clothing, bloody and broken with a bone sticking out of one leg.

Ittuq came closer and poked at the ijiraujaq with the barrel of his rifle and it didn't stir. He pushed the body onto its back, wondering why it hadn't attacked him yet. Its face was covered in scrapes and muck, its mouth hanging open. The eyes of the creature opened slowly, showing surprisingly white sclerae. It almost looked human....

The thing reached up at him and he brought his rifle up to aim.

"Eeetuuuuh," said the monster.

Ittuq's finger on the trigger hesitated. His instincts told him to get it over with, but something stopped him. There was a familiarity about this one. The ijiraujaq hadn't made any attempts to attack him, so Ittuq knelt down to peer at its face. He had nothing left to lose. The ijiraujaq's eyes closed tightly, squeezing out tears, and its mouth moved slightly. Ittuq looked close in the dim, lingering light and took the chance: he reached out to wipe the blood, dirt, and tears away from its face.

"Ittuq," she sobbed.

"Aliisa?" Ittuq started with recognition. Shaking, he said, "Aliisa! What happened? How did you get here?" He took her in his arms, looking over her body that was so broken it was almost unrecognizable.

Aliisa sobbed into his arm as he hugged her close. She'd made it back to him.

"What about Anirniq?" he asked. "Where is he?"

Her eyes squeezed shut. "I tried," she cried. "I tried so hard! I thought...I thought..."

Waves of relief and grief took over Ittuq. He nodded in stoic acknowledgement, not letting his feelings show. "It's okay, Aliisa, you did really good. You made it back; I've got you now." He held his hand on her shoulder, grateful for being together again. "Let's get you back to camp."

Aliisa visibly relaxed, tension easing from her overexerted body. Her lone struggle across the tundra was over. She knew Ittuq would protect her and take care of her until she had healed physically, and they would support each other until the emotional pain of losing another loved one faded slightly, day by day.

He looked over her injuries, assessing the terrible state she was in, and tried to make her more comfortable. He tied her leg with fabric to stop it from jostling. Next, he took his *qulittaq* off, tied its sleeves together, and slung Aliisa's body onto his back. A makeshift carrier to *amaaq* his precious cargo.

Everything had changed inside of him. The black shadows that had taken root in his mind faded away. He lit up with the changed circumstances; Aliisa needed him, and he would do anything to help her. The vicious conditions they lived in had taken two children away but given one back. And Ittuq would take what he could in a world with rare and sparse gifts. He happily accepted the life he was given: Aliisa's and his own.

He walked with new purpose across the tundra with Aliisa on his back, feeling like he could carry ten of her. The last hints of light faded behind them.

"We're both going to be okay," he whispered into the chilly air.

Glossary of Inuktitut Words

Notes on Inuktitut pronunciation

The pronunciation guides in this book are intended to support non-Inuktitut speakers in their reading of Inuktitut words. These pronunciations are not exact representations of how the words are pronounced by Inuktitut speakers. For more resources on how to pronounce Inuktitut words, visit inhabitmedia.com/inuitnipingit.

Word	Pronunciation	Definition
Aaliq	AH-leek	name, meaning "laugh until they almost can't breathe"
agluit	AHG-loo-eet	seal breathing holes
ai ja ja ja ja	ah-EE jah jah jah jah	a traditional musical refrain
aippaq	ah-EEP-ahk	spouse
Ajak	ah-YAHK	aunt (mom's sister)
akuliaq	ah-KOO-lee-ahk	between the eyes
amaaq	ah-MAHK	carry in an amaut
amaut	ah-MAH-oot	woman's parka with a pouch for carrying a child (traditional spelling)

amautaliit	ah-mah-oo-tah-LEET	a race of ogresses who wander the tundra looking for children to snatch
amauti	ah-MAH-oo-tee	woman's parka with a pouch for carrying a child (modern spelling)
amautiit	ah-MAH-oo-teet	plural form of "amauti"
anaana	ah-NAH-nah	mother
Anirniq	ahn-EER-neek	name, meaning "spirit" or "breath"
ataata	ah-TAH-tah	father
ataatatsiaq	ah-TAH-taht-see-ahk	grandfather
atigi	ah-TEE-gee	coat or parka. Traditionally, an inner skin parka with the fur side in.
atiq	ah-TEEK	word meaning "name"
Gwich'in	gwich-IN	an Indigenous group from the Northwest Territories and Alaska; also the name of the language spoken by these people
huva?	hoo-VAH	what?
Igali	ee-GAH-lee	name, meaning "person with a stove"
iglu	EEG-loo	snow house

igluit	EEG-loo-eet	plural form of "iglu"
ijirait	ee-YEE-rah-eet	shape shifter
ijiraq	ee-YEE-rahk	shape shifters
ijiraujait	ee-YEE-rah-oo-yah-eet	zombies (similar to an ijirait)
ijiraujaq	ee-YEE-rah-oo-yahk	zombie (similar to an ijiraq)
Immak	eem-MAHK	name, meaning "to put water into a container"
inua	EE-noo-ah	a being or spirit attached to the sky, wind, or an object
Inuit	EE-noo-eet	plural noun meaning "the people;" a group of Indigenous peoples from the Arctic regions of Alaska, Canada, and Greenland
Inuk	EE-nook	singular form of "Inuit"
Inuktitut	ee-NOOK-tee-toot	Inuit language
Inuvialuktun	ee-NOO-vee-ah-look-toon	Inuit language of the Inuvialuit people, an Indigenous group from the Canadian Arctic
Ittuq	ee-TOOK	name, meaning "grandfather"
kamiik	kah-MEEK	two skin boots

kitturiat	keet-TOOR-ee-aht	mosquitoes
kuniit	KOO-neet	kisses given by placing the nose on a person's face and breathing in
mamaqtuq	mah-MAHK-took	delicious
mikku	mee-KOO	dried caribou
nàhgą	NAH-gah	Tłįchǫ word meaning "bushman"
nuka	noo-KAH	younger sibling of the same sex
nukaq	noo-KAHK	little sister or brother of the same sex
nuna	noo-NAH	land
nungusuittuq	noo-NGOO-soo-eet-took	that which never ends
palaugaaq	pah-lah-oo-gahk	bannock
pana	pah-NAH	snow knife
panik	PAH-neek	daughter
Pualuk	poo-ah-OO-look	name, meaning "mitt"
qajaak	kah-YAHK	two kayaks
qallunaat	kah-loo-NAAT	white people
qavvik	kahv-VEEK	wolverine
Qiluya	kee-LOO-yah	name, meaning "someone pulled up"
qinngummivik	keen-GOO-mee-veek	look out hill

qiturngaak	kee-TOOR-ngahk	someone's two children
qulittaq	koo-LEET-tahk	caribou skin parka (fur side out)
qulliq	KOO-leek	seal oil lamp
taaliqtuq	tah-LEEK-took	it's now dark
taaqsivalliajuq	tahk-SEE-vahl-lee-ah-yook	getting dark
taaqtumi	tahk-TOO-mi	in the dark
taikungaunngilluti	tah-EEK-oo-ngah-oon-ngee-loo-tee	don't go there
taima	TAH-ee-mah	the end; stop
tarniq	tahr-NEEK	soul
tarralikisaaq	tahr-RAH-lee-kee-sahk	butterfly or moth
tarraqtuut	tahr-AHK-toot	mirror
tarriaksuit	tahk-REE-ahk-soo-eet	a race of peaceful, invisible beings
tuktu	TOOK-too	caribou
Tusaaviit?	too-SAH-veet	Are you listening?
Tusaqsauvungaa?	too-SAHK-sah-oo-voo-ngah	Can you hear me?
ujarak	oo-YAH-rahk	rock
ukaliq	OO-kah-leek	Arctic hare
ukaliqsiuqtunga	OO-kah-leek-see-ook-too-ngah	hunting Arctic hare

Ukkusiksalingmiut	ook-KOO-seek-sah-leeng-mee-oot	Indigenous group from the Back River area of Nunavut
ulu	OO-loo	crescent knife traditionally used by women
upanngillugit	oo-PAH-ngee-loo-geet	don't approach them
utiqtuq	oo-TEEK-took	returning; going back
utirululaurit	oo-TEE-roo-loo-lah-oo-reet	go back
utsuuk	OOT-sook	vagina

Contributors

Jessie Conrad is a member of the Yellowknives Dene First Nation. Her life philosophy is to confront your fears head-on, a principle reflected in her creative writing practice. "I Wouldn't Miss Them" is her second publication. She continues to write stories based on the authentic experiences of Indigenous women in the Northwest Territories. Her Instagram handle is @jessieceline22.

Jamesie Fournier enjoys exploring his culture through writing. Born and raised in Denendeh, Jamesie lives and works in Iqaluit, Nunavut. His debut horror, *The Other Ones*, published with Inhabit Media, won silver at the 2022 Independent Publisher Book Awards. His poetry collection, *Elements*, was shortlisted for the 2024 Indigenous Voices Award and won the 2024 NorthWords Book Award. Fournier's writing has been published in various magazines and anthologies, and the edited volumes *Coming Home: Stories from the Northwest Territories* and *Ndè Sı̀ı Wet'aɂà: Northern Indigenous Voices on Land, Life & Art*. Jamesie was consulting producer for the 2024 Iqaluit CBC Massey Hall Lecture and his premiere children's book *Lemming's First Christmas* was released for the 2024 holiday season.

Micah Silu Inutiq is an Inuk mother of two, born and raised in Iqaluit, Nunavut. From a young age, she has been fascinated by Inuit stories and all that they have carried through generations of life on the land. When not reading and writing, Silu enjoys spending time on the land with her family, drawing inspiration from her roots. With a lifelong passion for Inuit mythology and artistry, she is thrilled to share her first contribution to the *Taaqtumi* anthology with readers.

Aviaq Johnston is an Inuk author who grew up in Igloolik, Nunavut. She has written the award-winning novel *Those Who Run in the Sky* (2017) and its sequel, *Those Who Dwell Below* (2019). Since winning the Indigenous Arts and Stories Award for her short story "Tarnikuluk" in 2014, Aviaq has explored many different styles of fiction writing, including children's picture books, young adult novels, short stories, and screenwriting for film and television. She lives in Iqaluit, Nunavut, with her dog, Sunny.

Gayle Uyagaqi Kabloona is Ukkusiksalingmiut (from the Back River area north of Baker Lake, Nunavut). Now based in Ottawa, she is interested in blending traditional Inuit storytelling with science fiction and magic realism to create alternate realities. Gayle is an emerging writer and multidisciplinary artist with a focus on fibre arts, ceramics, and printmaking.

Malcolm Kempt spent seventeen years living and working in Nunavut. His short fiction was long-listed for The Best Horror of the Year (Volume 16, 2023). His debut Arctic thriller, *A Gift Before Dying*, is set to be released by Crown Publishing (Penguin Random House) in January 2026. He currently resides on the island of Newfoundland.

Terrie Kusugak is an artist of multitudes; she performs as a musician and singer, specializing in traditional drum dancing and contemporary music, and she is also a writer and beader. During summer months she spends her time at her parent's cabin and winter months inside reading and playing cards with friends. Kusugak is also a stand-up comedian who has a lot to say about the North. She currently resides in her hometown of Rankin Inlet, Nunavut.

Rachel Qitsualik-Tinsley was born at the northernmost edge of Baffin Island, in Canada's Arctic. She grew up learning traditional survival lore from her father. **Sean Qitsualik-Tinsley** was born at the southernmost edge of Ontario. He grew up learning traditional woodcraft. They were brought together by a love of nature and each other. Together, they write Arctic speculative fiction and nonfiction for various ages.